SALOON SHOWDOWN

"You son of a bitch," Lester Smalley said. "Hoyt's my friend. Don't you go hittin' him."

"Friends don't try to kill each other," Calhoun said flatly.

"That's none of your affair neither. Now get yourself out of the way while me and Hoyt tend to our business."

"Be glad to," Calhoun said. "Soon's one of you coughs up some cash."

"Go to hell, boy," Smalley snapped.

Calhoun pasted Smalley a powerful shot to the face, and the farmer went down in a bloated heap. Calhoun turned to look at Hoyt Jameson, who was just ramming the last ball home in the five-shot pistol.

With shaking hands, Jameson brought the pistol up in Calhoun's direction, jerking back the hammer with his thumb.

"Don't do it," Calhoun said harshly.

"Kiss my ass, you interferin' son of a bitch." Jameson began aiming.

"Goddamn fool," Calhoun muttered.

ALSO BY CLINT HAWKINS

SADDLE TRAMP
THE CAPTIVE
GUNPOWDER TRAIL
GOLD AND LEAD
BANDIT'S BLOOD
SIOUX TRAIL

COMING SOON

DEATH RIDES IN TEXAS

Published by
HarperPaperbacks

ATTENTION: ORGANIZATIONS AND CORPORATIONS

Most HarperPaperbacks are available at special quantity discounts for bulk purchases for sales promotions, premiums, or fund-raising. For information, please call or write:
Special Markets Department, HarperCollins Publishers,
10 East 53rd Street, New York, N.Y. 10022.
Telephone: (212) 207-7528. Fax: (212) 207-7222.

SADDLE TRAMP

HORSE THIEVES' TRAIL

—————————— ✦ ——————————

CLINT HAWKINS

HarperPaperbacks
A Division of HarperCollinsPublishers

This is a work of fiction. The characters, incidents, and dialogues are products of the author's imagination and are not to be construed as real. Any resemblance to actual events or persons, living or dead, is entirely coincidental.

HarperPaperbacks   *A Division of* HarperCollins*Publishers*
10 East 53rd Street, New York, N.Y. 10022

Copyright © 1994 by HarperCollins*Publishers*
All rights reserved. No part of this book may be used or reproduced in any manner whatsoever without written permission of the publisher, except in the case of brief quotations embodied in critical articles and reviews. For information address HarperCollins*Publishers*,
10 East 53rd Street, New York, N.Y. 10022.

Cover illustration by John Thompson

First printing: February 1994

Printed in the United States of America

HarperPaperbacks and colophon are trademarks of HarperCollins*Publishers*

❖ 10 9 8 7 6 5 4 3 2 1

CHAPTER
* 1 *

Wade Calhoun was sitting in a sinkhole of a saloon called the Pig's Blood Inn, minding his own business when a stray bullet shattered the whiskey bottle on the table inches from his right hand. "Shit," he mumbled as he flinched a little.

Calhoun had been watching a ruckus between two men since the beginning. He had no idea what had started it. The men had been drinking together, seemingly peaceful, when they suddenly began exchanging harsh, loud words. Their voices had continued to increase in intensity and volume, but Calhoun still had not thought much of it, since the two had the look of farmers.

The two had shoved up from their table, looking ready to start swinging fists at each other. That's when Calhoun noticed they were packing pistols, which he thought rather odd. It also gave him a few moments' concern, since farmers were notoriously poor shots with handguns. Or so he had always thought.

Before he could do anything, though, the farmers had drawn their pistols and were plugging away at each other. One of those bullets had shattered Calhoun's whiskey bottle, and he knew it could've very well been him instead of the glass.

1

The two finally ran out of ammunition, and Calhoun stood, his pockmarked face burning in an angry scowl. Calhoun was not a big man—about five-foot-ten and one hundred sixty pounds—but his lanky, wiry frame belied the strength in his long, ropelike muscles. He was as hard as a slab of granite and as powerful as a fiery preacher roaring against the evils of sin in a place like the Pig's Blood. Cold blue eyes peered out fiercely from a lean, hawklike face beneath a worn slouch hat. He was, all in all, a fierce-looking man.

Calhoun stalked forward to where the farmers were hastily trying to reload their old, five-shot, cap-and-ball Colt Patersons. A man of few words, Calhoun said simply, "You boys owe me a bottle of rotgut."

"Huh?" one of the farmers asked, looking up from his reloading in surprise.

"You heard me," Calhoun said calmly.

"What'n the hell're you talkin' about, mister?" the other farmer asked.

"The marksmanship from you two idiots sent some lead through my whiskey bottle. One of you—or both—owes me another."

"You're crazy, mister," the second said.

Both farmers had stopped their reloading and were staring at Calhoun as if he really were crazy.

Calhoun shrugged. He wasn't about to tell these two that he was down to his last three dollars and couldn't really afford another bottle on his own. Not that he really needed another bottle, but since he had paid for the other, he figured he was due a replacement.

"Get the hell out of here, mister," the second farmer said.

"Yeah, this ain't your affair, pal. Get going," the other added.

Other saloon patrons, who had taken cover when lead started flying, began rising from behind tables or from the floor and gathered around the three men, though not too close.

"You fools tryin' to kill yourselves ain't my affair. Your killin' my bottle of whiskey is." Calhoun paused, then shrugged. "Give me the few bucks for another, you can shoot at each other all goddamn day for all I care."

The farmer nearest Calhoun gave him a shove with his left hand. "Just get the hell out of my way, pal," he growled.

Calhoun glared at the man, taking stock. His opinion was not favorable. The farmer was an inch or two shorter than Calhoun but more substantial in size where girth was concerned. He wore a homespun shirt and pants, and his hat was even more battered and disreputable looking than Calhoun's. His plain work boots were covered with mud and pig dung.

Calhoun suddenly snapped a fist out, catching the man in the snout. The farmer, being of substantial heft, did not fall, but he staggered back a few steps.

"Hey, goddammit," the other farmer snarled, "you can't do that to Lester."

Without a word, Calhoun took two steps. As the nervous farmer raised his hands to protect his face, Calhoun thudded a punch into his stomach. The man's hands dropped, and Calhoun hammered him once in the face.

The farmer, being considerably smaller than either Calhoun or Lester, went straight down onto his seat, eyes dazed.

"You son of a bitch," Lester Smalley said. "Hoyt's my friend. Don't you go hittin' him."

Calhoun turned to glower at Smalley. "Friends don't try to kill each other," he said flatly.

"That's none of your affair neither. Now get yourself out of the way while me and Hoyt tend to our business."

"Be glad to," Calhoun said. "Soon's one of you coughs up some cash."

"Go to hell, boy," Smalley snapped in what he figured was a voice to frighten anyone.

Calhoun sighed at life's many little, though ubiquitous, annoyances—like Smalley and his friend. He walked to Smalley and punched him twice in the face.

Smalley dropped his pistol, all of a sudden urgently wanting to bring his fists into play, to protect himself. He looked like a fat man, but he was strong, and he figured that if he could either hit Calhoun a few good licks, or maybe get him in a bear hug, he would prevail. Trouble was, the doing was a lot more difficult than the imagining.

Calhoun didn't bounce around or dance. He simply moved forward as he pushed Smalley back by pounding on Smalley with relentless efficiency.

Smalley finally managed to land a few shots, but they were devoid of power, and Calhoun hardly noticed them.

Calhoun at last pasted Smalley a powerful shot to the face, and the farmer went down in a bloated heap. Calhoun turned to look at Hoyt Jameson, who was just ramming the last ball home in the five-shot pistol.

With shaking hands, Jameson brought the pistol up in Calhoun's direction, jerking back the hammer with his thumb.

"Don't do it," Calhoun said harshly.

"Kiss my ass, you interferin' son of a bitch." Jameson began aiming.

"Goddamn fool," Calhoun muttered. His hand moved in a blur, and suddenly one of his two Colt Dragoons was in his right hand and aimed. He hesitated only a heartbeat, as he saw Jameson start to pull the trigger. He fired just once.

The .44-caliber lead ball banged through Jameson's face and head, shattering his left cheekbone on the way in. Jameson's head snapped backward with the impact, and he fell, dead before he hit the ground. His finger jerked reflexively on the trigger, and his pistol fired.

Calhoun shook his head in annoyance again as he caught in his peripheral vision a man to his right falling, hit by Jameson's wild shot. "You bastard!" he heard from behind him. He started to turn and felt—or maybe heard—a bullet whine past him. He crouched and sped up his spin, bringing up the Dragoon.

Smalley had gotten a pistol from somewhere and was cocking it to take another shot when Calhoun spotted him. Calhoun fired twice, aiming for Smalley's bulbous torso. At a range of less than ten feet, there was no way he could miss such a large target. Both balls hit Smalley in the chest, ravaging his heart and at least one lung. He crumpled with a sighing groan.

Standing where he was, Calhoun turned in a slow circle, angrily checking out the saloon patrons. None posed an immediate danger to him. The one Jameson had accidentally shot was dead, and another was wounded. Calhoun supposed the latter had been shot accidentally by Smalley.

Seeing that no one seemed to be ready to bother him, Calhoun went and knelt alongside Smalley's body and began going through his pockets. He found two dollars and seventy-nine cents. He went to Jameson's corpse and began doing the same. He had just pulled out a small pile of paper money when he heard, "Hold it right there, mister."

Calhoun glanced up as his hand went for a pistol.

"Don't be a damn fool," a tall, gray-haired, hard-looking man said quietly. The drawl in his voice was thick. The man had a jawful of chaw, carried a short-barreled shotgun, and wore a tin star on his shirtfront.

Calhoun nodded and eased his hand away from the revolver. He stood at the lawman's command.

"I'm J.C. Scruggs, town marshal of Pleasantville. Now, drop the money, then ease out both your pistols and that giant hog sticker of yours, and drop 'em down on poor ol' Hoyt there."

"I was only defendin' myself, Marshal," Calhoun said.

"I ain't conversin' with you, son, till your fangs're pulled. Now lose the weapons."

Calhoun nodded and dropped the money. He pulled the Dragoons out of the cross-draw holsters one at a time, using only thumb and forefinger and dropped those, too. Next his big bowie knife went. He was more concerned about Scruggs's shotgun than he was about keeping his pistols. Besides, he figured that even if Scruggs arrested him, Calhoun still had his backup weapon on him—he had a Colt Walker with the barrel cut down to two inches resting in a small holster at the small of his back under his shirt. It was a devastating weapon at close range.

Scruggs relaxed very little, though he did move his finger off the scattergun's trigger and let it rest alongside the trigger guard. It let Calhoun know that the marshal wasn't about to just gun him down, but it gave Calhoun no room to cause trouble. "Now, son, suppose you tell me just what the hell all this here carnage is about."

"This ass and his friend over there," Calhoun said, pointing to Jameson and then Smalley, "were arguin'. They unlimbered their weaponry and . . ."

"Y'all ain't gonna try'n tell me they shot each other down and you was just lookin' for some pocket money, are you, son?" Scruggs said skeptically.

"No, sir," Calhoun said seriously. "These two couldn't hit anything they were tryin' to hit. One of their stray shots broke my bottle, and came damn close to hittin' me. I come over while they were reloadin' and told them they owed me a new bottle of rotgut."

"Is that a fact?" Scruggs still sounded skeptical.

Calhoun nodded. "They tried to give me a hard time, so I punched the fat one over there. He tried comin' back at me so I kicked the shit out of him. By then, this skinny one had reloaded and was fixin' to shoot me in the back. I got him first. As he fell, he fired and hit that poor son of a bitch over there." Calhoun pointed again.

"Then?" Scruggs was beginning to believe Calhoun. He had seen men like Calhoun before, and such men did not go around shooting down unarmed saloon patrons, or even armed farmers for no reason.

"Somebody gave chubby back there a pistol and he corked one off at me. Hit that bastard." Calhoun pointed to the wounded man. "Then I put him out of his misery." He shut up, then, having said more in the past few minutes than he had in the past month.

"Anybody dispute those facts?" Scruggs asked.

"I do, Marshal," one man said, stepping forward. He had the unmistakable brand on his face of a full-time drunk, a man who would do anything if he thought it'd get him a drink.

"Shut up, Lyle," Scruggs said. He risked taking his eyes off Calhoun for a few moments and scanned the room. No one seemed willing to speak up. He looked back at Calhoun. "Reckon you're tellin' the truth, son. Or at least enough of it. But I'm still gonna ask y'all to take yourself elsewhere."

"Now?"

"Yes, sir."

"These two still owe me for a new bottle. I took two bucks and change off the fat one. I figure another two dollars or so from this one"—he tapped Jameson's body with the toe of his boot—"ought to make us square."

"Keep the money you took from Lester." He glanced to the bar. "Curley, bring a bottle over for this feller. What's your name anyway, son?"

"Wade Calhoun."

"Well, Mister Calhoun, step back from Hoyt's body there a few paces." When Calhoun had, Scruggs said, "Billy, get his pistols and bring 'em to me." Scruggs took them one at a time and stuffed them into the copious pockets of his short coat. He waited until Calhoun was holding the bottle of whiskey in his hand, then said, "All right, Mister Calhoun, outside. And please, son, don't y'all try nothin' foolish. There's been a far piece more killin' in Pleasantville today than was needed. I'd hate to add you to the total."

Calhoun nodded and headed outside, slamming a shoulder into one man who thought to challenge him on the walk. The man fared the worse for the brief confrontation.

Just outside, Scruggs asked, "Where's your horse, son?"

Calhoun pointed to a belligerent-looking pinto nearby.

"Nice lookin' horse," Scruggs commented.

Calhoun shrugged. He had never had any luck at all with horses and so he never formed any attachment to any particular horse. He generally was satisfied enough with whatever animal he had at the time. He walked to the horse and mounted it.

"Damn, that's some fine saddle y'all got there, son," he said with a low whistle. "Where'd you get it?"

The saddle was Calhoun's only real possession, other than his pistols. He was proud of it. It was a Mexican-style saddle of heavy leather inlaid with silver filigrees and such. The horn was as large as a small dinner plate, and large, fancy *tapaderos* covered the fronts of the stirrups.

"From a Mexican general," Calhoun said flatly.

"You killed him?"

Calhoun nodded.

"During the war?"

Calhoun nodded again.

"I fought with General Taylor myself." Scruggs eased down the hammers on his shotgun, and squinted up at Calhoun. "You give me your word you won't use your pistols agin me?"

Once more Calhoun nodded. He took his pistols as Scruggs handed them to him and slipped them into the holsters.

"I got nothin' agin you personally, son," Scruggs said. "But I think it wise if y'all was to give Pleasantville a wide berth in the future."

Calhoun touched the brim of his hat, turned his horse, and trotted away.

CHAPTER
* 2 *

Calhoun seldom had any specific destination when he rode out—or was run out, which was more often the case—of a town. This time was no exception. With no place to really go from Pleasantville, Missouri, he considered riding west into Kansas Territory. But that thought saddened him, for Kansas Territory was where he had gone from being an army scout, loving husband, and devoted father, to the wandering saddle tramp he was now. He sighed with pain, as he did every time he remembered the burned-out farmhouse, and the ghastly bodies of his dear Lizbeth and their lovely little daughter Lottie.

He stopped to roll and light a cigarette, hoping the actions would help him blot out the memories, at least for a little while. He finally started riding again, turning generally southwest. Texas had been good to him at times in the past, or at least less bad than many other places he had roamed, and that seemed as likely a place as any to go now.

A couple of hours later, he pulled to a stop in a thicket along a small river. The place had wood and water and forage for the horse. He decided to spend the night there, even though it was barely afternoon.

He did his chores—tending the horse, gathering firewood, starting a fire, cleaning the pistol he had used back in the Pig's Blood—then cooked what little salt beef and beans he had left. He didn't eat it all, though.

After eating, he got the bottle of whiskey he had acquired at so great a cost, and proceeded to drink the entire thing over the next several hours. He sipped at it strongly and steadily, smoking innumerable cigarettes in the doing. He did not even know when he fell into a drunken stupor, and probably wouldn't have cared even if he had known. Death meant nothing to him. He almost welcomed the thought at times, since that would bring him relief from the memories that haunted him every day.

He felt like hell the next day, as he knew he would, and he grumped around his camp, groaning and swearing at himself for his foolishness. He polished off the last of his beef and beans and then lost it all when his stomach revolted at it.

Along about noon, he roused himself enough to drink the last of his coffee and then saddle his horse. Disgusted with himself, he pulled into the saddle and rode on, hoping to find a town so he could get some supplies. When he thought of the three dollars that was all the money he had, he wondered how he could get supplies. Seven dollars sure wouldn't get him very far. He thought about that as he traveled.

Late that afternoon, he rode into a place named Oak Ridge, a pretty-looking town, one so nice looking that it almost set Calhoun's teeth on edge. He stopped at a restaurant and used seventy-five cents for a decent meal. Then he wandered to the Post Oak, a saloon that looked disreputable enough for him to enjoy. There was something about a rancid saloon—one that smelled of flat beer, rotgut whiskey, old tobacco, and even death—that made him feel right at home.

The Post Oak wasn't quite that bad, but it was still Calhoun's kind of place. Without much money, he ordered two shots of rye and a mug of nickel beer. He downed the shots of whiskey one right after another, enjoying the jolt they sent through his system. Then he shoved some dead-asleep drunk out of a chair and took a table where he nursed his beer, trying to decide what to do about some cash. He was not above rolling some drunk, though that usually proved to be a decidedly inadequate way of building any kind of stake. There was gambling, but he had little to start with.

Part of the way through his third beer, and having downed two more shots of rye, Calhoun decided that he would wait till midnight and then simply break into the general store and take what he needed. Decision made, he relaxed and paid a little more attention to the people around him. Not that he cared about them, but he was a wary man and one could never tell who might cause trouble. On occasion, some high-rolling gambler might win a pile of cash and then get drunk. Such a man was easy pickings for a man like Wade Calhoun.

No such gambler was in existence in the Post Oak, but Calhoun did begin to focus in on a man who kept spouting off about how good a pistol shot he was. The man was taller than Calhoun by a little, and as thin and razor-faced. Where they differed, though, was in dress. Where Calhoun was clad in battered hat, filthy, threadbare shirt, and worn denim pants, the man at the nearby table wore boots almost to the knee; a long, swallowtail coat, crisp, boiled shirt without a collar, and good, wool pants. Calhoun figured that the hat sitting on the table near the man cost nearly as much as his own pinto. The man had a small group of men—plus two prostitutes—clustered about him, hanging on his every word. Or so it seemed to Calhoun.

Calhoun sat listening a little, growing angrier and nastier by the minute as the man's puffery grew more and more grandiose. Finally he could stand it no more. The alcohol had made him slightly tipsy, but that did not bother him. He didn't know how he had acquired the propensity for being able to shoot as well when stone drunk as he could when sober. All he knew was that it was true.

Once on his feet, though, he steadied and walked calmly over to the other table. He shoved between a trollop and a man and slapped down some money. "I wager that—which is all the money I got—plus my horse that you're full of shit."

The man looked at Calhoun. His face wrinkled with disdain as he took in Calhoun's clothes and the harsh, pocked face. "You know who I am, boy?" he asked after several seconds.

"Nope. Don't give a shit neither."

"I'm Claude Hopkins, and I'm the best goddamn pistol shot on either side of the Mississippi River." He smiled an oily smile. "You sure you want to challenge me, boy?"

"That all you can do is shoot off your mouth?" Calhoun asked with a sneer.

Hopkins's face colored with choler. "I don't bet for such small amounts, mister," he said harshly.

"What's the matter, boy, you can't cover my wager?"

Hopkins looked like he was about to choke on his

own venom. "You've asked for it now, you ugly son of a bitch," Hopkins snarled as he pushed himself up. His swallowtail coat flapped open some, showing two Allen and Wheelock pistols. "Pick your target, damn you."

"How about we just shoot at each other?" Calhoun asked with a slightly mocking tone.

Hopkins bit back a retort. "Barkeep," he called. "A couple of silver dollars over here." When the bartender had brought them, Hopkins said, "Stick them sideways into the chinks in yonder wall." He pointed.

The bartender did so and stepped back. "Well, now, boy," Hopkins said with a sneer, "let's have at it, shall we?"

Calhoun nodded.

The two moved forward, stopping when they were about twenty feet from where the silver dollars were stuck in the wall.

"I'll take your wager this time, friend," Hopkins said, "just seeing if you can hit either one of those coins."

"What're you puttin' up?" Calhoun asked calmly.

"I'll match your cash, however little it is, plus throw in two double eagles."

Calhoun nodded, whirled, drew, and fired. Then he held out his other hand. "I'll take those double eagles now," he said in the same even tone he had used a moment ago.

"Sweet Jesus," a saloon patron said loudly. "Hit that son of a bitch square on, he did."

An excited murmur rippled through the assembled group of men.

"To hell with that," Hopkins snapped. "I ain't shot yet."

"You said the first one was all mine," Calhoun said quietly.

"All right, dammit," Hopkins said angrily. "Double or nothing. I'll hit the other."

Calhoun shook his head and held out his hand. "My cash."

"Now, wait a minute, mister," Hopkins said in what he hoped was a friendly tone. "You got to give me a chance to win back my money."

"No I don't," Calhoun said reasonably. "But I will. Bartender, let's use a couple of half dollars this time." He turned back to Hopkins. "We both fire this time."

"We keep shooting until one of us misses?"

Calhoun shrugged and nodded. "But first, my winnings."

Hopkins reluctantly handed Calhoun two twenty-dollar gold pieces.

The two fired slowly, one at a time, allowing a saloon regular named Harry Barker to check the coins after each shot. Five shots each later, the coins had been driven so far into the wall that they could no longer be seen.

"Let's make this a little more interesting," Hopkins said, having regained his confidence and cockiness. "How much're you willing to put up?"

"Same as before, plus the forty dollars I won. You?"

"Well, seeing's how you're putting up about all you own, I'll make my wager a bit larger. One hundred dollars, cold, hard cash."

"You got that much on you?"

"You impugn my honor, sir," Hopkins said with wounded dignity.

Calhoun tossed his hat on a nearby table and ran a hand through his shaggy mop of light brown hair. "You ain't got it, and the last shot'll be the one I put through you," he said quietly.

Hopkins nodded, accepting, but he had suddenly become a little pasty of face. He called the bartender and had the man use two nickels this time. "Think you can handle that, boy?" he asked, looking at Calhoun.

Almost casually, Calhoun half turned and fired.

"Got it square!" Barker shouted.

Hopkins fired and hit the coin. Then Calhoun and he alternated. Hopkins missed on his fourth shot, and blanched when Barker announced it.

Calhoun uncocked his Colt but kept it in his right hand. He held out his other hand. "My cash," he said harshly.

Hopkins laughed self-consciously, hoping that Calhoun would relax his vigilance a moment so he could use the last shot in his Allen and Wheelock to dispatch this damn saddle tramp. But he could see in Calhoun's snapping, blue eyes that such would not be the case. "I . . . heh, heh . . . don't actually have that much on my person, you understand. I . . ."

"Where is it?" Calhoun asked roughly.

"Over in my room. It's right down the street. I'll go get it and come right back."

"I'll just go with you," Calhoun said in a voice that let Hopkins know he would brook no argument about it.

Hopkins nodded, crushed.

"After you," Calhoun said. He grabbed his hat and slapped it on. He followed Hopkins out, keeping the Dragoon in his hand, just in case, carrying the pistol at arm's length down his right leg.

Hopkins turned toward his room from the side staircase of a small hotel. He unlocked a door and went in, with Calhoun right behind him. "It's right over here in a box," Hopkins said, kneeling on the far side of the bed. His hand reached for a pistol he kept there next to a small lock box. He hesitated when he heard the cocking of Calhoun's pistol. He left the revolver on the floor and picked up the box. There was no way he wanted to test Calhoun's gun hand at this close distance after the demonstration Calhoun had put on at the Post Oak.

Hopkins stood and set the box on the bed. He unlocked it and pulled out five double eagles. It left him with only one twenty-dollar gold piece. Suddenly he flung the five coins at Calhoun and he ducked, going for the gun under the bed.

Calhoun fired, putting the ball into the floorboards near Hopkins's left hand. "I've got one more in this pistol, and five in the other. You still want to tempt fate?" Calhoun asked coldly.

"No," Hopkins muttered into the floor.

Calhoun moved up behind him and knelt with one knee on Hopkins's back. He placed the muzzle of his Dragoon lightly against the back of Hopkins's head. With his other hand, he took the pistol on the floor and threw it on the bed. Then he got one of Hopkins's Allen and Wheelocks and threw it after the first. He took the second pistol from Hopkins's holster, flipped it in his hand, caught it by the barrel, and then whapped Hopkins hard on the back of the head. Hopkins didn't even have time to groan before he was unconscious.

Calhoun stood and tossed Hopkins's last revolver on the bed. Then he uncocked his own pistol. He reloaded it with paper cartridges taken from a hard leather pouch on his gun belt. With the Colt back in its holster, Calhoun picked up the five gold coins and put them in his pocket. Then he checked the box on the bed. Seeing only one more coin in there, he also pocketed that. He figured Hopkins owed it to him for all the trouble he had caused.

Shrugging, Calhoun looked around the room some more. He found some fashionable clothes, like those Hopkins was wearing, but he decided they were not for him. The only other thing he took from the room was a pint bottle of whiskey.

He swiftly left the hotel and walked up the street to his horse and walked it across the street to the general store. Taking his saddlebags inside, he bought himself some beans, bacon, salt beef, jerky, coffee, horse grain, and cigarette fixin's. Outside, he threw the saddlebags across the horse and tied them down. He mounted up and headed off.

Before he got out of town, though, he heard a hiss from a corner of a building. Glancing at the alley, he saw one of the prostitutes who had been sitting with Hopkins. He rode there.

"Did you kill him?" she asked.

"What makes you think I'd kill him?" Calhoun countered.

"There was a gunshot, and we all saw how good you were with that pistol of yours," she said nonchalantly. "I figured he'd try somethin' foolish, too. He was that sort."

"Yes he was," Calhoun agreed. "Well, good day, ma'am." He turned the horse and moved off.

"Hey," the woman shouted, "don't you want me?"

"No," Calhoun said flatly. He rode away.

C H A P T E R

* 3 *

Calhoun rode throughout the rest of that day, made a small camp, and then rode all the next day and the day after that. He didn't really think that a man as pompous as Claude Hopkins would have made many friends in Oak Ridge, but he couldn't be sure. For all Calhoun knew, a posse could be on his trail right now.

That, of course, was nothing new to him, he acknowledged sourly. It seemed as if he were always in the wrong place at the wrong time and was getting mixed up in affairs that were not really his business. He was often blamed for things that were not his fault, especially if violence was involved. Years ago, when he first took to tramping around the West after Lizbeth and Lottie died, such things bothered him. But no more. Indeed, if he were a humorous man at all, he would've thought many of his situations funny.

Because he thought a posse might possibly be out after him, he skirted the few towns and farms he came upon. A few days more of traveling that way, without trouble, and he figured he was safe. He caught a ferry across the Arkansas River and pulled into Fort Smith, Arkansas. It was a bustling place, with plenty of saloons—some good, some bad—hotels, and brothels and cribs. With the activity on the Arkansas River, and the army post of Fort Smith just outside town, all these amenities got pretty good use.

Calhoun left his horse at the first livery stable he found. Then, carrying his saddlebags over his shoulder, he headed down the street. He found a hotel, got a room, and then went to the nearest dry goods store. There he bought himself a new outfit—nothing fancy, just a plain, cotton, collarless shirt, new denim pants, a couple of bandannas, some socks. He figured that his hat and boots could stand some more wearing. He found a tonsorial parlor, had a bath—his first in quite some time—as well as a decent shave, and had his unruly locks trimmed a bit. Then he went to a restaurant where he took care of the largest beefsteak he could find, plus potatoes, beans, and then a heaping portion of apple pie.

Sated with food and good feelings, he headed to his hotel. Finding the proprietor, Jake Bancroft, he asked, "You know which of the whorehouses around here is the best?"

Bancroft never raised an eyelid. A man like Calhoun—young, tough, and unmarried—would be expected to look for such a place as soon as he rode into town. "Most expensive is Sweet Annabelle's. Up two blocks and over one. Big, brick place. You can't miss it."

"Sweet Annabelle's?" Calhoun asked, cocking an eyebrow.

"It ain't what you think," Bancroft said with a chuckle. "Annabelle's about sixty, maybe more. The name comes from her being a sweet old lady."

Calhoun nodded. "Anything a little cheaper but still good?"

"Sure. Fat Chester's. He owns a saloon and attached brothel, plus cribs out back, and some action upstairs in the saloon. Over on Fifth Street. Then there's Thelma Thorne's over on Grand." He looked around to make sure his wife was not in listening distance. "Tell you the truth, Mister Calhoun, Thelma's got the best girls. All young, but not too young. All pretty and all know how to treat a man just right. There's a saloon next door, too. The Rosebush. Word is that Thelma owns that, too, but silently."

Calhoun nodded and left. While he usually preferred dank saloons and low cathouses, there were times when he preferred something a little fancier. This was one of those times. He found Thelma's with no trouble and hesitated only a moment before heading inside, after deciding that a stop at the Rosebush could wait a while.

A surprisingly young woman—about thirty, which was mighty young to be the owner of such a place—greeted him just inside the door. She was short and slim and attractive, and fully dressed in severe clothing. It left no doubt that she among all the women here was off limits.

"You must be Miss Thorne," Calhoun said pleasantly.

The woman looked up into that harsh, almost-handsome face and shuddered a little from its inherent force. She met such men all too rarely, despite the nearby presence of an army post and all the tough men wandering through here on their way to hell. "I am," she finally said, after taking a few moments to recover her senses.

"I've heard you got the best place in town."

"I like to think so," Thelma said with pride. She smiled a little. "You want to give me a name? Or would you as soon be like the others and just use a first name, probably not yours."

"My name's Wade Calhoun," he said almost arrogantly.

"Pleased to meet you, Mister Calhoun," Thelma said, still fighting the animal attraction of this tough-looking customer. "Now, come with me."

Thelma led him to a sitting room. He was the only one in there except for Thelma. "Want something to drink, Mister Calhoun?" Thelma asked.

"Rye. Neat. Thank you."

Thelma poured it and handed it to him. "Now, Mister Calhoun, we really prefer that our clients don't wear their side arms around here."

"Sorry, ma'am. They'll come off when it's time for me to get down to business."

Thelma hesitated a moment before saying anything. Wade Calhoun was not the first man who had ever refused to take off his guns before she brought her girls out. That's why she had Court McVey and his four assistants. McVey was a big man, tough as tempered steel and quite handy with a handgun, but Thelma wasn't sure he could handle Calhoun. It would be an interesting matchup, she figured.

Thelma nodded. "If you insist," she said softly. She smiled a little. "Do you have a preference, Mister Calhoun?"

"As to what, ma'am?"

"Hair color, size, build . . . or perhaps you have a . . . pleasure that might not be . . . shall we say normal?"

"No, ma'am, nothin' like that. An acquaintance says you got the prettiest girls and they all know how to treat a man good. If that's true, then I'll be happy."

"I assure you it is true, Mister Calhoun. Well, one more drink perhaps before I get the girls?"

Calhoun nodded.

While Calhoun sipped at the short glass of whiskey, Thelma left. She returned with four other women. Bancroft had been right. All were young—older than seventeen, but younger than twenty-two, he guessed—and all were quite pretty. They were demurely, if not overly dressed. All were well-proportioned, bright-eyed, and smiling. Two were white, one black, and one looked like some kind of Indian. Calhoun dismissed the latter in his mind right off. The way he felt about Indians, he could not see himself lying with one, no matter how attractive she might be.

The black woman had small, firm breasts and was tall and quite thin. Her nose was widely splayed, and her kinked hair was cut very short. Both of the white women were short. Where one was a little plump, the other was rather thin. The plump one had long, light-brown hair; the other's was a dark chestnut.

"This is a hell of a hard decision," Calhoun said. Though he did not smile, the women seemed to know that he spoke the truth. He finally stood and pointed to the plump white woman. Something about the way she smiled, or the way she looked at him made him believe she would be almost as interested in the night's activities as he would be.

The three other young women filed out. Thelma nodded. "Now, Mister Calhoun, before Miss Grace takes you away, there are some of the more mundane matters to get out of the way." Thelma was all businesslike now. "How long were you planning to stay with Miss Grace?"

"Till I figure I'm done."

Grace giggled and quickly choked it off when Thelma cast a dark look at her. "That's not very humorous, Mister Calhoun."

"Wasn't meant to be. It's been a time since I been with a woman, especially one as fine as Grace. I might not be done with things in a half hour or hour." He paused and pulled a double eagle out of his pocket. "Tell you what. You hold this." He handed Thelma the coin. "When I leave, you can figure what I owe and take it out of that."

Thelma smiled and nodded. "As you wish, Mister Calhoun. Enjoy yourself."

"I aim to, ma'am."

Grace's room was sparsely furnished, though nicely appointed. The bed was spacious and looked comfortable. Grace turned down the quilt and the top covers. She turned and smiled at Calhoun. "Well, Mister Calhoun, what's your pleasure?"

"My first pleasure'd be for you to call me Wade."

"All right, Wade. Then what?"

"I think the both of us have a heap too many clothes on for what we're about to be doin'."

"I agree." Grace began unbuttoning the bodice of her simple dress.

Calhoun left around midnight, twelve dollars lighter, but feeling considerably better about life. Not great, mind you, but about as good as he ever felt about himself. Grace had either been as willing as he had thought she would be, or she was a better actor than any Calhoun had ever seen in a theater. He had no trouble getting to sleep once he got back to his hotel room that night.

In the morning, Calhoun decided that he would stick

around Fort Smith for a while. It was a pleasant enough town, but the main reason was that he wanted to explore the women over at Thelma Thorne's some more. He wanted to experience Grace's bubbling passion again, and find out exactly how Daphne, the other white, and Esther, the black, responded to him.

He figured he had enough money to last him at least a few weeks of high living, if that's what he chose. Which he didn't. The only high living he did was spending a fair number of hours at Thelma's, and occasionally going to the Rosebush. Most of his saloon time, though, was spent in the Arkansan, a hellhole of a place. It was more than foul enough to suit Calhoun.

In the next week, he spent plenty of time at Thelma's. He learned that Grace indeed was as bubbly as she seemed. He also learned that Esther was equally passionate, though quite reserved in showing it. That was not what he had expected from a black woman, considering some of his boyhood experiences back in Tennessee. Daphne turned out to be cold and wooden, at least with him.

Within another week, Grace and Esther felt that Calhoun was their best customer ever. And they told Thelma so.

"Why?" Thelma asked, though she was not really surprised.

"Well," Grace said, "unlike most—well, hell, all our other customers—Wade cares about us. Or at least he does me. He wants to see that I have a good time, too."

"Yes'm," Esther added. "He do that fo' me, too."

"He does have a certain attraction, I suppose," Thelma mused, thinking back to her initial meeting with Calhoun. "I might even have to sample him myself one day."

For his part, Calhoun was beginning to entertain notions of maybe settling down in Fort Smith. The people were friendly enough, and he felt fairly sure he could get himself a job as deputy county sheriff, or maybe deputy town marshal—constables they called them here. If not, there were other things to do. He had a number of years' experience as a scout for wagon trains and the army. He could do that from here, too, what with the army post being right outside town. Stagecoaches rode through here all the time, and could probably use a good shotgun rider. And there were freight wagons heading into Texas all the time. Most any one of them would be glad to have another gunhand along as protection against the Indians and thieves.

But things had a way of going wrong for Wade Calhoun, and he damn well knew it. Even as he entertained ideas of settling down in Fort Smith, he was waiting for some trouble to arise, since he figured it was inevitable.

That did not stop him from enjoying himself as much as he could. He gambled at poker and faro, drank among the dregs of Fort Smith in the Arkansan, and visited Thelma's place. He managed to stay out of fights and gunplay, but he was sure that sooner or later his hand would be forced, and his peaceful days in Fort Smith would be over.

He never really expected trouble at Thelma's, though. She had several hard-fisted, well-armed men who kept the peace at her brothel, as well as in the Rosebush saloon next door. In addition, her prices were higher than many other similar places in town, meaning that the soldiers rarely, if ever, could afford to go there. She also kept the customers apart as much as possible, bringing them into one or another of the sitting rooms by themselves, getting them set up with a young woman and then bringing in the next. Of course, on busy nights, sometimes that precaution had to be overlooked simply because of the volume. And, finally, she limited the amount of whiskey the customers could have. Two drinks of whiskey generally were considered sufficient. On occasion, she might allow a favored customer—one like Calhoun—to indulge a little more freely in the alcohol, but it was rare indeed that a man got drunk there. Or even tried to get inside when he had imbibed too much elsewhere before showing up at Thelma's. Court McVey and his crew were quick to toss such offenders into the street.

Calhoun went over to Thelma's most nights. He would banter as much as he was able with her before disappearing with Daphne or Esther. A few times, though, Thelma had hinted that she might be available to him, but she always seemed to withdraw from him, as if afraid.

Thelma Thorne wanted Calhoun. It was not love or anything close to it. Just a desire to have for a short time a man whom she was sure would excite her. Every time she saw him she felt a twinge of excitement of the same sort she felt when she was in danger. That's what held her away from him as much as it pushed her toward Calhoun.

Finally she relented, and stopped Calhoun as he was leaving one night. "If you were to consider dropping by here again tomorrow night, there might be someone . . . special? . . . waiting."

"The only special one around here I know of is you, ma'am. I'll be here."

CHAPTER

* 4 *

Calhoun was surprised to find four soldiers in the hallway of Thelma Thorne's, waiting to get into one of the sitting rooms and pick themselves a woman. One was a lieutenant, fairly young and fresh-faced. The other three were upper-rank sergeants, men with fire in their eyes and twenty years of army cooking in their bellies. They were a tough-looking crew.

Calhoun shoved past the soldiers and headed down the hall to the back kitchen where McVey and his crew made their headquarters on busy nights. McVey wasn't there, but one of his men, Milt Eichorn was.

"Christ, am I glad to see you, Calhoun," Eichorn said with a sigh.

"What the hell's goin' on?" Calhoun asked.

"It's one of those nights we have every now and again. Once in a while, the soldiers seem to think they want to come on over here instead of goin' to their usual dives. Then it gets crazy."

"Where's Court?"

"At the Rosebush, I think. Things're crazy over there, too. Jesus, you think you could help out around here a bit before takin' your pleasures?"

29

"I suppose I . . ." He stopped when he heard a scream. He was already running when he heard Eichorn say, "That's Thelma."

As Calhoun churned down the hallway, he saw that two of the burly sergeants had Thelma pinned up against the wall. One was trying to kiss her; the other had his hands roaming over her body. Calhoun heard the latter say, "Now come on, Miss Thelma, we been in the army too long to have to wait to mop up on them bitches you got upstairs. You're here, we're here, and we got the goddamn money, so what say you . . ."

Calhoun slammed a shoulder into the sergeant on the near side, sending him thudding against his companion. Both fell. Calhoun did not. He swept Thelma behind him with a protective arm.

"That was a dumb move, you harebrained son of a bitch," the third sergeant said. He started reaching for his pistol.

"No!" one of the sprawled soldiers said. "That piece of shit is mine. Don't nobody knock Sergeant Paul Thatcher on the ground and try'n take his woman," he said as he got up. "Now, you scrawny little fart, let's see just how much gumption you got." Thatcher spit on his hands and rubbed them together. He looked almost happy.

Calhoun was tempted to just shoot the loud-mouthed Thatcher down here and now, since he was in a hallway against a man who outweighed him by a fair amount and who by the look of him had been in many a brawl, and probably hadn't lost too many of them. But shooting the fool wouldn't go over very well, so he waited. "Milt, get Thelma out of here," he ordered.

"Don't you take that woman nowhere, you pissant little skunk," Thatcher growled. "As soon as I rip this asshole's head off, I'm gonna finish my business with her."

"Get her out of here, Milt," Calhoun said. He took two quick steps forward, feinted a punch at Thatcher's head, and then lambasted him one in the stomach instead.

Thatcher doubled over, but he didn't stay that way for long. But in those few instants, Calhoun dipped his hand into his belt pouch and grabbed his small pouch of lead pistol balls. Wrapping it in his fist, he walloped Thatcher in the jaw as the sergeant straightened.

"Jesus goddamn Christ," Thatcher said, the words garbled by his newly broken jawbone.

Calhoun did not wait nor talk. He simply moved forward a step and pasted Thatcher several shots in the face and head with a lead-supported fist.

Thatcher finally fell, landing on his side with a trembling groan.

The other sergeant who had been accosting Thelma had gotten up and as soon as Thatcher fell, he charged at Calhoun. He barreled into Calhoun, knocking him back and down, landing half atop him.

With the fist holding the ball pouch, Calhoun slammed punches into the soldier's side and head. The sergeant—Curtis Williamson—managed to get in a few licks, too, but they had little leverage.

Calhoun managed to shift himself up onto his side just a little, and then force Williamson over. They rolled again, until Williamson's back hit the hallway wall. Calhoun jabbed a thumb into Williamson's throat and pushed as hard as he could.

Williamson gargled and slammed the heel of a hand on Calhoun's forehead, snapping Calhoun's head back.

Calhoun broke away from Williamson and rolled twice. Then he got up, chest heaving. As Williamson began rising, Calhoun kicked him under the chin.

"Bastard," the third sergeant yelled. Once again he went for the revolver in his flap holster.

Calhoun had had about enough of these soldiers. From his work with the army, he generally liked soldiers and got along with them. Not this particular bunch, though. He dropped the small buckskin sack of lead balls and ripped out of one his Dragoons. He could see no reason to hesitate. He pumped a ball into the sergeant's chest, and then added another one for good measure.

Thelma heard the gunshots and raced out of the kitchen, heading down the hallway. Eichorn was right behind her. They got to Calhoun just in time to see him gun down Lieutenant Al Peters. The officer had been foolish enough to think that he could somehow draw his pistol from the flap holster and shoot down Calhoun, before Calhoun, who still had his pistol in hand, could get him. All for revenge of a sergeant he did not like all that much anyway. He was wrong. Dead wrong.

"Dear God, Wade," Thelma breathed.

"It had to be done."

"I know. But now we've got to get you out of here and out of Fort Smith."

"She's right, Wade," Eichorn said. "The commander over at the fort's gonna go wild when he hears about this. He'll tear the town apart lookin' for whoever killed his men."

"My runnin' won't help," Calhoun said.

"Like hell," Thelma snapped. "We'll just tell him it was some drunk we've never seen before."

"What about those two?" Calhoun asked, pointing to Williamson and Thatcher.

"They don't know we know you. We'll tell him the feller come in, saw two of his sergeants manhandling me and came to my rescue. When he gunned down those two, he ran off. Went west, followin' the Arkansas."

Calhoun nodded. He had no desire to face off against an entire fort full of soldiers. And he had known his life in Fort Smith had been too good to last.

"Milt," Thelma said, "go get Court and the others. Tell 'em I don't care what's going on over at the Rosebush, I want them back here now." When Eichorn had taken off, Thelma turned to Calhoun. "Get to my room. Top of the stairs on the right. Stay there till I come and get you."

"But . . ."

"Don't argue, Wade. There's a lot to be done yet."

Calhoun shrugged and went up the stairs. He sat in a chair near the window, looking out over the city. He would've been despondent had this not been the way his life had gone since the Sioux had raided his place in Kansas Territory and Lizbeth and Lottie had been . . . He cut that thought off before it grew into something unwieldy. He rolled a cigarette and lit it and then prowled the room, looking for some liquor. He finally found a bottle and went back to the chair. He sipped slowly while puffing on cigarettes, waiting.

Less than half an hour later, Thelma came into the room. She smiled ruefully. "We could've had some good times here," she offered. Then the wan smile dropped. "Your horse is saddled and out back. Your saddlebags are packed and on the horse. There's a few days' supply of food."

Calhoun nodded, accepting it, not caring how it had been accomplished.

"I don't know which way you were headed when you came into Fort Smith, Wade," Thelma said, "but I'd head out in any way other than west along the river." She hesitated. "You better get movin', Wade."

Calhoun nodded. He stood, squashed out his cigarette and headed for the door. He stopped when Thelma called quietly to him.

She walked up and planted a powerful kiss on his mouth. When she broke away, all she could find to say was, "Damn."

Then Calhoun was out the door and heading down the stairs. Court McVey and Milt Eichorn nodded as he headed for the kitchen, and the back door.

He continued his original course going southwest, with the vague goal of reaching Texas, deciding what he would do then.

He rode hard for a while, not believing that Thelma and her people would be able to forestall a search for him. Too many people in that small brothel knew him, and knew that he had been visiting there regularly. He wasn't sure if he had even mentioned to Thelma, Daphne, or Esther that he had been heading for Texas. He didn't think so. He was not a man prone to gabbing in general, and for a while there he had been thinking of staying in Fort Smith. That he might have mentioned, but that wouldn't help the army anyway.

Still, there was no guarantee that the commander of Fort Smith would believe Thelma or any of them. There was nothing much west of Fort Smith except Indian country. A lot of men would think to run that way, figuring that the army would not want to head into those strange lands. On the other hand, a man could lose himself in Texas fairly easily, if he wanted, since that state was so large.

He finally spit into the dirt. Such thoughts were getting him nowhere. Either the army would come this way or it would not. Either the army would believe Thelma or not. Either the army would catch him or it would not. Worrying about it would not affect any of those things. Riding long hours, however, might have an effect on those things. So he rode well into the night, then stopped for just an hour to let the horse rest, He took the time to clean the revolver he had used back at Thelma's. His guns had seen him through a lot, and he made his way in life with them. Because of that, he took excellent care of them. Done with that, he tightened his saddle and rode on again.

By morning, he was feeling some of the effects of too little sleep. He stopped again and built a small fire, made some bacon and beans and coffee. He ate slowly, then had two more cups of coffee and a cigarette. He finally rose and wearily saddled the pinto and left.

It began to rain sometime during the morning. As he rode, Calhoun could see the storm blowing in, and when he figured it wasn't far off, he pulled on his long slicker. He worried about tornadoes and hail, which were common in these parts, especially at this time of the year. The wind howled and blew but did not turn into a twister. The temperatures plummeted, but no hail appeared. It just poured bucketsful, while lightning spat and crackled, and thunder reverberated off the Ouachita Mountains that he was rapidly approaching.

By midafternoon, Calhoun figured he was beyond pursuit. At least for a while. It would take the army a couple of hours to gear up to send out a patrol after him, if the commander had decided it was necessary, and there was no end of directions he could've gone. Even if the soldiers guessed right and headed this way, they would've started out a few hours behind him, and they would've stopped for the night last night, putting them another eight to ten full hours behind. Besides, if they were tracking him, the rain would've slowed them down even more.

Calhoun pulled into a small wooded area abutting a stream running through the low western edge of the Ouachitas. It was still raining, and Calhoun was exhausted. All he wanted to do was sleep, but as much as he hated having to do it, he unsaddled and tended the horse. Finished, he hobbled the animal and then he sat. Deciding that he did not care about eating, he stretched out his bedroll under a small tree and slid in between the blankets wrapped with waterproofed canvas. He was asleep in moments, oblivious to the still-pouring rain and the crashing thunder.

It had stopped raining by the time he woke not long before dawn. He arose, annoyed that he would have to go searching for firewood, then try to build a fire on sopping ground. Growling a little, he began the search. By the time dawn was edging into the little grove, he had a fire going and coffee heating. After two cups of coffee, he figured it was time to make his breakfast, which he did with little flourish and less expectation.

Finally he got back on the trail, the pinto's hooves slopping through the muck. The sun came out, warm and fierce, but it still took two days before the land was dry again.

Calhoun continued riding southwest, keeping a little off the stage trail or anywhere else he thought there might be travelers. He also avoided any towns and farms he came across, deciding that he did not need the trouble they brought.

Six days after he had ridden out of Fort Smith, though, he was certain he was safe, and he was almost out of supplies. He stopped in a small town he found, resupplied and rode straight out again, forgoing even a stop at the only saloon in the town, which didn't have a name as far as he could tell.

Two afternoons later, Calhoun stopped to give the horse a break. He moved a few steps away and rolled a cigarette. He had just flicked the match away after lighting it when the hobbled pinto let out a frightened squeal. Calhoun whirled, hand reaching for a pistol, but the horse seemed to be all right. In fact, the animal was lowering its great head to forage again. Baffled, Calhoun watched for a few moments.

When the horse whinnied in fright this time, Calhoun saw the reason—a six-foot-long rattler had struck, sinking its fangs into the pinto's nose.

Calhoun spit as he brought out a pistol. "Shit," he muttered. Snakes did not frighten him, but he did not particularly care for them either. He was angry now since he figured he'd be afoot before long. Calhoun walked forward slowly, eyes alert. He spotted three rattlers, and he dispatched them with three quick shots. He quickly slit the rope hobbling the horse and walked the animal away. Lord knew, there might be some more snakes around, and he was in dire enough straits as it was.

CHAPTER

* 5 *

Calhoun saw no more snakes, which was a relief, but the pinto's muzzle soon began to swell. Calhoun knew of nothing he could do to help the horse, short of bleeding it to try to get out some of the poison. He figured that, though, would cause the horse more pain than it was already in, and he wasn't sure it would do any good. His only hope was that the snake had not injected too much venom in the horse. With the pinto's nose being mostly cartilage, the venom wouldn't go through it too quickly. Not like it would if the snake had bitten into muscle.

Calhoun looked back every few minutes, especially after the pinto began slowing down, jerking on the reins. The animal's muzzle kept swelling ever larger. Before long, Calhoun stopped and removed the bridle, bit, and reins. He hung them on the saddle and took his rope. Placing a loop around the horse's neck, he used the rope to tow the animal along.

Within an hour of getting bitten, the horse's face and head were swollen up so much that its eyes were closed and its nostrils almost shut off. The horse was having trouble breathing, and so it couldn't walk too well. It stumbled and lurched.

"Whoa," Calhoun finally said, stopping. He turned and walked to the animal and patted it on the neck and then shoulder, feeling sorry for it. He usually didn't much care for whatever horse he had, considering his poor luck with them, but he didn't like seeing this one suffer. It had been a good horse, all in all.

He pulled off the fancy Mexican saddle and dropped it and the saddle pad on the ground. With a bit of reluctance, he drew a Dragoon and shot the horse in the head. As the animal fell, Calhoun jerked the loop of rope off. He coiled the rope as he watched the pinto's last desperate jerking struggles before dying.

Annoyed and angry, Calhoun squatted and rolled a cigarette. He smoked it down, trying to keep his mind blank. As he squashed the cigarette butt under the toe of his boot, he rose, mind made up. He could go back to the town where he had resupplied, but that would take him two days or more on foot. He had no idea how near a town or farm was in any other direction. His best bet, he figured, was walking toward the road where the Butterfield stage ran. He might have to hunker down and wait a couple of days when he got there, but a stage would come along sooner or later. He had a few days' worth of supplies, so he could last a while.

With a sigh, Calhoun hoisted the heavy saddle, made heavier by the Henry rifle, the 10-gauge shotgun, and the supplies of food. He left the saddle pad and the bag of horse grain behind. He headed south and west, moving slowly but steadily across the rolling hills. Being late spring, the land was bright and green, though that would taper off somewhere to the west as one reached the short-grass prairie, which in turn gave way far to the west to a more barren land, one that was desert to most who traveled its trackless and almost waterless wastes. Wildflowers stretched out to the horizon except to the east, where the low Ouachita Mountains grew.

It took Calhoun almost three days of walking before he caught a glimpse of the stage road from a grassy ridge. No stage, or even the dust from one was visible. Neither was sight of a relay station. Calhoun found a pleasant, shady little spot along a stream amid tangles of brush and trees, and he set up his camp, prepared to wait.

He was running out of food three days later when he finally heard the rumble of a stage. He kicked dirt over his fire, grabbed his saddle, and moved across the stream and up the ridge. Across the road, the land was much like it was here, cut through with coulees, rolling hills, and thickets.

Calhoun stopped, dropped the saddle, and then flopped down when he spotted two mounted men working through another little gully to his left. When they were out of sight around a bend, he stood and picked up his saddle again. Then he followed them down in the gully, which bent and then meandered at an angle that would bring them out right near the stage road. The stage would have little choice but to stop if the men were out there to rob it, which Calhoun suspected they were.

Even in the little gully, which was thick with brush, Calhoun could hear the sound of the approaching stage. He hurried a little, stopping when he saw daylight ahead. The two men were sitting just to the side of the road, bandannas over their faces, guns drawn.

Calhoun edged up as close to the road as he could while still being screened by brush. He stopped behind a cottonwood. Keeping the saddle slung over his shoulder, he eased out one of his Dragoons and then he, too, waited.

The rumble of the approaching stagecoach was quite loud now, and Calhoun knew it was close. He was tempted to go out and remove these two men now, but then decided that would be foolish. It was possible, he supposed, that they weren't planning to rob the stage, but he could see no other reason they would be out here with masks on their faces. More importantly, though, if he did dispatch them now, the stage driver just might figure he was one of the robbers.

"Whoa up there!" one of the men yelled. The stage stopped.

Calhoun knew now for certain that it was a robbery.

"You," the robber nearest Calhoun said, pointing at the shotgun rider, "toss down that scattergun and your side arm."

The man did.

"Throw down the mail pouch," one of the robbers commanded. From his position, Calhoun could not be sure which one of the men had spoken.

When the canvas bag was tossed down, the robber farthest from Calhoun dismounted and picked it up. He handed the bag to his partner, who held it and his reins in his left hand. Then, while the mounted robber kept his pistol trained on the driver and guard, the other opened the stage door and ordered everyone out.

Calhoun figured he had seen enough. Still holding his saddle over his shoulder, he cocked the Dragoon and walked quietly out of the gully. When the driver spotted him and raised his eyebrows, Calhoun held the gun to his lips as a sign that the driver should keep silent.

Calhoun moved up right behind the mounted robber, whose back was almost straight in his direction. He looked at the other. "Hey, you!" Calhoun shouted.

The robber removing valuables from the passengers glanced over there, saw Calhoun and began turning. Calhoun shot him in the head, and the man fell.

The gunshot spooked the other robber's horse. The animal reared, and the robber tumbled to the ground. His horse went racing off, followed by the other robber's animal. The mail bag dropped to the ground a few feet from where the robber landed hard.

Calhoun moved up right away, and placed a boot on the robber's chest, keeping him pinned to the ground. He pointed the cocked Colt at the man's face. "I believe this robbery is at an end," he said quietly. He glanced up at the driver and guard. "What do you want to do with him?" he asked.

The guard swiftly clambered down and retrieved his weapons. He tossed the shotgun up on the seat and holstered his pistol before stalking around the horses to where Calhoun still held the robber down. "Let 'im up," the guard growled.

Calhoun moved his foot and stepped back a pace.

The robber rose, and the guard yanked his mask off. "Well, well, well," the guard said. "If it ain't Rudy Schell."

"You know him?" Calhoun asked.

The guard shrugged. "Know of him. The bastard's robbed more than his share of stages along the Butterfield line." He pointed at the other robber's body. "I expect that'll be Dexter Lee. They usually work together."

Calhoun nodded, no longer concerned. He watched Schell while the guard went to get some rope to tie

Schell up with. When the guard returned, Calhoun walked toward the body and the passengers. He still carried his saddle, but he slid the Dragoon away.

The guard went behind Schell with the rope. As he began pulling one of Schell's arms back to tie it, Schell suddenly jerked the elbow back and then immediately did it again. As the guard's breath whooshed out, Schell went for his belly gun.

Calhoun dropped his saddle and whirled, jerking out his pistol again. "Drop!" he roared at the guard, who was between him and Schell. When the guard did, Calhoun and Schell fired at the same time. Schell's bullet hit the stagecoach with a solid thunk, while Calhoun's blew a hole in Schell's chest.

Calhoun glanced down at the first man he had shot, and noted that he was dead. Then he checked on Schell, as the guard rose shakily.

"Goddamn, that was close," the guard said with a nervous chuckle. He held out his hand. "Joel Hawthorn," he said. "And I'm mighty obliged to you for what you done here."

"Me, too, mister," the driver said. He had wrapped the reins around the brake handle and climbed down just a moment ago. He, too, held out his hand. "Frank Osgood."

Calhoun nodded and shook each man's hand. "Wade Calhoun. You ain't obliged to me, but if you're willin', I could use a ride to the next station or town."

"Hell, we'll do more'n that, boy," Osgood said with a laugh. "We'll stand you a beefsteak supper and a bottle of the best rotgut we can find soon's we get to Cross River." He smiled at Calhoun's blank look. "It's right across the Red River in Texas."

Calhoun nodded again. "You got room for my saddle?"

"Sure," Osgood said. "What happened to your horse?"

"Snakebit. His head and face got so swole up he couldn't breathe, so I shot him."

Osgood grimaced in sympathy. "Well, we best bury them two boys," he said.

"Why?"

Osgood and Hawthorn looked at Calhoun in surprise. "But they deserve . . ."

"Go ask your passengers if they think those two bastards deserve a decent burial," Calhoun said flatly.

Hawthorn went to protest again, but Osgood cut him off. "Mister Calhoun's right. Besides, Joel, we got us a schedule to keep."

"I suppose you're right, Frank," Hawthorn said. He moved off. "All right, folks," he said in a strong, sure voice, "this unpleasantness is over with. Go on and get back aboard. We'll be leavin' directly." He started helping people inside the coach.

"You're about to become a rich man, Mister Calhoun," Osgood said.

Calhoun raised his eyebrows in surprise and question.

"The stage company's offerin' a reward for those two jaspers."

"Can't be a hell of a lot."

"I expect no more'n a hundred each. Maybe less. Still, them's pretty good wages for a driver, so to me it makes a man rich. For a spell anyway."

Calhoun would not take the bait. "Reckon I could use that money. Get me a new horse."

Osgood was disappointed, but he got over it right away. He was not a man to remain gloomy for long, especially when he had just had his life saved by this man. He figured coming out of this alive and with all his passengers intact and the mail untouched was payment enough from Wade Calhoun. "It's too bad, though," he said, "that their horses run off like they did. You could've took both of 'em, and nobody would've said a word against it."

Calhoun shrugged. It had happened and all the wishing in the world wouldn't make it different.

Hawthorn walked back up to Calhoun and Osgood. "The other's Dexter Lee all right," he said. He smiled at Calhoun. "That's a hell of a saddle you got there, Mister Calhoun," he said.

Calhoun nodded. "You got room in the boot to store it?"

Osgood shook his head. "No, sir, we sure don't," he said with a little regret. "But we'll put it up top and tie it down good. I ain't expectin' no rain or other poor weather before we get to Cross River. If we do, we'll try'n figure out somethin' else." He shrugged, helpless to change things. "It's the best I can do."

Calhoun nodded. He turned, got his saddle, and waited next to the stage door. Hawthorn climbed up to the top of the wagon and reached out. Calhoun held the saddle as high as he could. Bracing himself on one hand, Hawthorn grabbed the saddle with his other. When he tried to jerk it up onto the stage, he almost tumbled off from the weight.

"Damn," Hawthorn muttered.

Calhoun lowered the saddle and looked up. "Maybe you best let me get up there," he said.

The two men changed positions. When Hawthorn held the saddle up, Calhoun grabbed it with one arm and hauled it up, then set it easily down on the coach roof. He stood there and watched as Hawthorn climbed up and lashed the saddle tightly down.

When he and Hawthorn had gotten down, Calhoun asked, "There room in the coach for me?"

Osgood nodded. "Might be a little cramped, but you can fit. Unless you'd rather ride up with us."

"Too hard to sleep that way," Calhoun said. He walked around and pulled himself into the coach, nodding at the people inside. He settled down between a flowery smelling drummer and a portly older man who had the look of a banker about him.

He looked across the coach at the three people there. On one side was a disreputable-looking man who seemed to be a gambler. Judging by the state of his clothes and his cleanliness, he wasn't a very successful one. On the other side was an oily looking man whom Calhoun figured was a bunko artist or something equally shady.

Wedged between the two was an attractive young woman, dressed primly and properly, with a fancy hat and simple though good-quality dress. Her hands were folded demurely in her lap, and a mass of golden curls poured out from under the hat. She looked at Calhoun only once, revealing deep green eyes, and smiled weakly before lowering her eyes again.

Thinking about the delightful young woman across from him, Calhoun slouched a little, pulled his hat down over his eyes, and proceeded to doze.

CHAPTER

* 6 *

Calhoun never did fall completely asleep. He heard the desultory talk that went on around him, and occasionally glanced out through slitted eyes. His mind filtered out what was important and what was not. Little was, other than the fact that the nice-looking young woman was being annoyed by the men on either side of her. That annoyed him, though it wasn't really his business. Still, he never did like seeing a woman treated poorly. Like when the two soldiers had attacked Thelma Thorne. He had not come to her defense because she was his, or because he loved her; no, he did it because he could not stand to see any woman, particularly one he liked, being abused.

They pulled into a way station just before dark, in a blowing cloud of dust and shouts. Two men came out of the rickety station, and a woman waited in the doorway.

Hawthorn jumped down from his perch up on the coach and opened the stagecoach's door. "Change of horses here, folks," he said. "Supper, too. Twenty minutes is all you have, so eat up fast. We'll be traveling through the night."

The gambler shoved up from his seat, almost rubbing his buttocks in the young woman's face in his

47

haste to get out the door. As the man was crouching to get out the door, Calhoun brought his foot up. Placing the sole of his boot against the gambler's rump, he gave a good shove. The gambler tumbled out of the coach, landing on his face in the dirt.

Calhoun looked at the woman, and waved a hand toward the coach door. "Ma'am."

"Thank you, sir," she said in a squeaky whisper. She rose and held out her hand so that Hawthorn, who was there to help passengers out, could take it.

Calhoun was next to the last out, and he moved away from the door and stretched. He hated being cramped up like that, but he decided it was a hell of a lot better than walking. He spotted Osgood talking to the two men from the station, who were swiftly unharnessing the horses. Osgood spotted Calhoun and waved him over.

"This here's the man I was tellin' you boys about," Osgood said when Calhoun got there.

The older of the two men stopped his work and reached out to shake Calhoun's hand. He was in his forties, with a seamed face and shock of gray hair that was fast dwindling. "Billy Kimball," he said. "That's my son, Benn," he added, nodding to the other man. The son was a twenty-year-younger and slightly larger version of the father.

Calhoun nodded.

"Frank tells me you stopped a robbery. Killed two outlaws in the doin', too." His clothes and person were filthy.

Calhoun nodded again.

"We had more men like you runnin' around, we'd have a heap less robberies," Kimball said. "Well, me and Benn got to get these horses changed, and I expect you're a hungry feller, Mister Calhoun. Go on inside and fill your belly. Mrs. Kimball's got a fresh batch of stew made up."

Calhoun headed for the house made of poor wood. Gaps were easily evident between the small logs, and no chinking had been used to close the holes. The inside was about what Calhoun had figured it would be—dim, dank, fetid. It was as bad as some of the jails Calhoun had been in.

If he thought the building itself was bad, the food was worse. Mrs. Kimball slapped something that looked like hog slop into a bowl. "Eat hearty," she said as she carried her stew pot back to the stove. Mrs. Kimball was a festering counterpart to her husband and son; a fat, slovenly, shapeless mass of womanhood with missing teeth, stringy hair, and hands that had not seen water in months, if not years.

"Coffee?" Calhoun said.

"It'll get there. Just set and eat. You ain't got much time."

"Now, now, Emma," Hawthorn chided from his place at the long table. "This's the man who killed them two robbers."

"Well, why didn't you said so?" Emma Kimball said, affecting something that Calhoun could only surmise was meant to be a warm smile. "Sit, mister, I'll bring your coffee right over." She was suddenly much friendlier.

Calhoun picked up his bowl and walked to the end of the table. "Move down," he said to the gambler, who was sitting on the end of the bench at the table, directly across from the woman passenger, who was next to Hawthorn.

The gambler looked up and was about to say something, but changed his mind. Even in the dark interior of the foul roadhouse, he could see the glint in Calhoun's eyes. With a low growl, he slid down the bench. Calhoun sat and glanced at the woman. She was looking at him with interest—and fear.

"How's the grub, ma'am?" he asked politely.

"Repulsive," she said in that breathy whisper that bespoke her fright. She grimaced at the remembrance.

Calhoun took a tentative spoonful and swallowed. He made a face. "You were too kind," he said, pleased when she smiled at him. "I'll tell you somethin'," he said in a conspiratorial tone. "Fill up on bread and leave the slop for the hogs."

The woman smiled again and nodded. Still, she suffered through more stew, trying to be polite to a fellow woman. She did, however, eat far more bread than she usually did, and was glad for the fullness it made her feel in her belly.

Calhoun had eaten food as bad, and worse, so he had no trouble plowing through the rancid meal. While they ate, Calhoun said to the woman, "Name's Wade Calhoun, ma'am."

"Pleased to meet you, Mister Calhoun," she said. "I wanted to thank you for stopping those robbers." She shuddered, remembering. "That one evil man was just about to take my wedding ring."

Calhoun nodded. He had seen the ring and had cast aside thoughts of perhaps having a rendezvous with this woman sometime. His hopes rose again somewhat with her next statement.

"It's almost all I have left from Johnny. The only thing personal, that is. There's the boardinghouse we ran together, but not much else of a personal nature."

"Sorry, ma'am," Calhoun said, at a loss for words.

"It's all right, Mister Calhoun. He's been dead more than a year now. I just visited his grave."

"You didn't take this stage ride just to do that, did you?" Calhoun questioned.

"Oh, no, Mister Calhoun." She smiled wanly, and Calhoun noticed the tiredness on her otherwise pretty face. "I had to go back to take care of some affairs— helping my parents. We buried Johnny back there, and so I went to see the grave while I was there."

Calhoun nodded.

"I've been running the boardinghouse myself since Johnny died."

"Where is it?"

"Cross River. Where're you heading, Mister Calhoun?"

Calhoun shrugged. "Don't rightly know, Miz . . .?"

"Oh, I'm sorry. I'm Irene McGowan. Where were you heading before you lost your horse?"

"Don't rightly know that either, Miz McGowan." He shrugged again. "Man like me doesn't have a home, nor anyplace to be in particular."

"Sounds like a lonely life, Mister Calhoun."

"I suppose it's that," he agreed. But he didn't like talking about himself and his spotty past. "You best eat up. They'll be boardin' again soon."

Calhoun walked with her outside soon after. Lanterns had been lit since darkness was almost upon them. "Would you be more comfortable sittin' next to me, ma'am?" Calhoun asked.

Irene looked up at him, then nodded. "I think I would, Mister Calhoun."

He nodded. "You go on and get in. Take the seat where the fat feller was sittin'. I'll be along directly."

Calhoun turned and waited just outside the door. In moments, the gambler came out, a piece of bread sticking out of his mouth. Calhoun grabbed him by the front of his fancy vest, swung him completely around and then slammed him back up against the side of the house. "Stay there," he ordered.

A moment later the banker came out, face flushed.

Calhoun stepped in front of him. "The young lady's sitting where you were," he said. "You take the seat directly across from her."

"But . . ." One hard look from Calhoun shut him up. He nodded.

Next out was the drummer, and Calhoun let him pass. When the bunko artist came out, Calhoun did the same to him as he had to the gambler. When both were up against the wall, looking frightened though trying not to show it, Calhoun said, "The young lady is unhappy with your attentions. I hear one more untoward word from either of you to her and I'll pound the shit out of you. And if either of you touches her again, I'll make goddamn sure you lose interest in all women for all time. You got that?"

"Just who the hell do you think you are, mister?" the bunko artist blustered.

"A friend of the young lady's."

"Just because you killed those two robbers doesn't give you the right. . . ." He shut up in a hurry when Calhoun pulled that big bowie knife and ran a thumb along one side of it.

"Just remember what I said, boys." He turned and walked away. When he entered the now lantern-lit coach, the flowery-smelling drummer was sitting next to Irene, looking pleased with himself. "Move," Calhoun said, pointing.

The drummer looked like he would swallow his tongue, he was so frightened. He swiftly slid along the bench and Calhoun took the seat between him and Irene.

Minutes later, lanterns on the coach were lit next to the driver and the guard. Then Osgood whistled and yelled, then snapped the reins. The stage lurched off.

Calhoun stretched out his legs, much to the annoyance of the bunko artist, who had gotten stuck in the middle of the opposite bench. Then Calhoun leaned his head back and pulled his hat down again.

"Mister Calhoun?" Irene whispered, feeling absolutely shameless. "Do you mind if I lay my head on your shoulder? I'm . . . I'm so tired, but I've been afraid to close my eyes."

"I don't know how comfortable my bony old shoulder's gonna be, ma'am, but have at it."

"Your shoulder's anything but bony, Mister Calhoun," Irene said with a smile. She felt odd about making such a personal request of a man she had just met. She reached behind the seat and pulled out two blankets. "One for you and one for me," she said.

"I don't need one, thanks, ma'am," Calhoun said.

"You sure?"

"Yes'm."

Irene folded one blanket to use as a pillow against Calhoun's hard-muscled shoulder. She spread the other out over her. Before long she was asleep.

Calhoun dozed again.

✳   ✳   ✳

The stage made two more stops that night, both times to change horses. Irene woke both times, but the first time she went right back to sleep. The second time, though, she roused herself and went outside to stretch and use the privy. Calhoun took the opportunity to get some fresh air and have a cigarette.

The next time the stage halted was at another way station just after dawn. Once again the horses were changed, and this time a meal was served. It was marginally better than the one they had at the Kimball's, but still left a bad taste in the mouth when it was over. There were two more stops in the morning, one just to change horses, the second to do that and to have a midday meal.

Finally, somewhere in the afternoon, the Red River hove into view, and soon they were stopped at Colbert's Ferry. It would be a little while before the ferry was ready to take them across the Red River, so Calhoun and Irene got out and walked around a little.

"Who's that?" Calhoun asked, pointing to a tall, stately, expensively dressed man with very dark skin.

"That's Mister Colbert. He owns the ferry."

"Looks like an Indian," Calhoun said flatly.

"He is. A Chickasaw. He's one of the richest men between Cross River and Fort Smith, though much, if not most, of the land belongs to the Choctaws."

Calhoun said nothing, but from the scowl on his face, Irene knew he was bothered. "Something wrong, Mister Calhoun?" she asked, hoping to pry it out of him.

"No, ma'am," he said with a sigh. "I just hate Indians is all."

"Did the Indians do something to you?"

"You might say that," Calhoun responded tightly.

"But Mister Colbert's not like other Indians," Irene said softly. "The Chickasaws are one of the five civilized tribes. They raise cattle and corn, just like everyone else around here. Many of them—including Mister Colbert—own slaves."

Calhoun nodded, not really trusting himself to say anything at the moment. Memories of a blazing farmhouse in Kansas Territory burned into his mind, as they had regularly ever since that day so long ago. Or was it so long ago?

Irene looked up at Calhoun as they continued walking. His face was as hard as stone, and she figured something terrible happened to him, done by Indians. She figured some of his family, or maybe some of his partners, had been killed by Indians. It was all too common anywhere out here, though Cross River was pretty well safe now. She decided that she ought not to mention that Benjamin Colbert, the rich Chickasaw, was on his third white wife.

Calhoun stopped, looking across the river. He could see the town of Cross River over there. It did little to improve his mood. He rolled a cigarette and lit it.

"I'm sorry, Mister Calhoun," Irene said softly.

He nodded. "You didn't do anything wrong, Miz McGowan," Calhoun said, looking at her a moment. Her bright, beautiful face was a stab of pain in his heart as he remembered Lizbeth, who had been every bit as beautiful as Irene McGowan.

Then Osgood called them, since the ferry was ready to leave.

CHAPTER

* 7 *

The stage left the ferry and then drove the half mile to Cross River. The town was set that far back from the river to avoid floods, Irene explained to Calhoun. Shortly after the town had been founded, the Red River flooded, and wiped out half the town's buildings. When it was rebuilt, it was moved away from the river a little.

Osgood stopped the stage in front of a building that had a brightly painted sign announcing it as the Butterfield Stage Office. Hawthorn climbed down and opened the door to help people out. "We'll be stayin' the night here in Cross River," he said. "Those of you goin' on'll leave in the mornin' with a new driver and guard. This's the end of the line for me and Frank."

Calhoun was the last off the stage, just after Irene. He stood and looked around. Cross River was a much more pleasant looking town than most out here in the middle of nowhere. Most of the buildings were of logs covered by false fronts. A few were made of brick. There were a number of saloons, several hotels, two dry goods stores, a hardware, the stage office, and quite a few other businesses that he could see.

"Hey, Calhoun!" Osgood called from up on the roof.

When Calhoun looked up, Osgood began lowering his saddle, using the rope that had tied it down.

Calhoun got it and untied the rope and tossed it aside. He nodded when Osgood called down, "Don't you go anywhere, Mister Calhoun."

"Well, Mister Calhoun," Irene said with a note of sadness in her voice, "I must be off to my boardinghouse. Perhaps we'll see each other again."

"I'd like that," he said honestly. "You take single-night boarders?"

"Why, yes. It's not usual, but I can do that."

"Well, I ain't goin' anywhere today or tonight for sure, so maybe I could take a room at your place."

"That'd be nice. It's over on Third and Comanche streets." She gave directions, then walked away, leaving behind a warm smile that lingered in Calhoun's mind, erasing for the moment the last of the bad memories.

Calhoun moved up onto the board sidewalk, out of the way of Osgood and Hawthorn, who were unloading the stagecoach. Calhoun watched Irene as she stopped and talked for a moment with a black youngster and then handed him a coin. She walked off, then, with Calhoun still watching. When Irene was out of sight, Calhoun set the saddle down and rolled a cigarette. He finished it just as Osgood and Hawthorn got done with the coach.

"Don't you boys have to load that thing all up again in the mornin'?" Calhoun asked as the two stepped up onto the boardwalk.

Osgood shook his head. "It's got to be loaded, but not by us. That's Charlie Endicott's job. His and Fred Waverly's. They'll take it on from here."

"Why unload it, though?"

"Mister Ferguson wants it that way," Osgood said.

"Henry Ferguson is the division superintendent," Hawthorn said. "He's in charge of all the stage line's operations between Fort Smith and Fort Belknap."

"He wants his coaches looking good, so at certain points, like Cross River," Osgood added, "he wants the coaches cleaned out and washed down."

Calhoun nodded, having gotten far more information than he wanted.

"Come on, Mister Calhoun," Osgood said after a moment, "I want to introduce you to Mister Ferguson."

They went inside the sparsely furnished building. In one corner was a ticket window at which worked an elderly man who looked bored and about ready to fall asleep. There were several benches scattered around the room, and a number of small, handcarts for luggage and packages. At the back was an office behind a closed door. The three men headed there.

Osgood rapped on the door and then shouted, "It's Frank Osgood, Mister Ferguson," when someone inside asked who it was.

The three went in, Osgood first, followed by Hawthorn and then Calhoun. They stopped in front of a large, cluttered desk. The man behind the desk was forty or so, and appeared to be tall, though it was hard for Calhoun to judge when the man was sitting. He was big of chest, and stomach, and looked like he might've once been a formidable man as far as strength went. Good living, though, had softened him. His hair was still full and dark, with only a trace of gray here and there, but his trim mustache was almost entirely gray. The rest of his face was clean-shaven. Bright, dark brown eyes were determined, a feeling emphasized by the thick eyebrows above them.

"Well?" Ferguson asked impatiently.

"This is Mister Calhoun," Osgood said nervously, pointing.

"Am I supposed to give a damn?"

"Yessir," Hawthorn said, slightly less tentatively than his partner had spoken.

"So tell me why," Ferguson said flatly.

"He stopped a robbery of the stage and shot down the two scum who were tryin' to rob us," Hawthorn said flatly. He was somewhat in awe of Ferguson, mainly because Ferguson held his job in his hands. That didn't mean he had to like it or that he had to kowtow to Ferguson all the time. Such subservience as Ferguson demanded was wearing on a man after a while.

"That true, Frank?" Ferguson asked, turning the deep brown eyes on Osgood.

"Yessir." Osgood felt the same as Hawthorn did about Ferguson.

"What'd he say your name was, boy?" Ferguson asked, looking at Calhoun.

"You always this big an ass?" Calhoun asked flatly.

Ferguson suddenly looked apoplectic. "Why you son of a bitch," Ferguson snapped, standing. His palms were on the desk, and he leaned forward, his weight on his hands. "Why I ought to . . ."

"Sit down and shut up before I knock you down."

Ferguson's eyes grew large in shock. No one ever spoke to him that way. "I don't have to take . . ."

"What you don't have is manners," Calhoun snapped, overriding Ferguson's protests.

Ferguson sat, mouth working furiously, though uttering no sounds. Finally he managed to control himself. He drew in a long, deep breath and then eased it out. Then he said, "You're right, Mister . . . Calhoun, did Frank say?"

The statement shocked Osgood and Hawthorn, but they said nothing.

"Sit, gentlemen," Ferguson said. "Please. And, Frank, you're the closest. There's cigars over on the sideboard there and whiskey. Have a drink, all of you, and a cigar. And some for me, too, Frank." Ferguson sat back in the chair, waiting until Osgood had poured drinks and passed around cigars. "All right, then, what happened?"

Osgood and Hawthorn explained it simply and quickly.

"You're sure it was Rudy Schell and Dexter Lee?" Ferguson asked when they were done.

Both stage employees nodded.

"Looks like you're due some cash, Mister Calhoun," Ferguson said, seemingly in better spirits than he had been a few minutes ago. "Let me see how much." He pawed through papers on his desk, until he found the two he wanted. "Here it is. Let's see, Schell had a hundred dollars on his head. Lee only fifty." He rummaged in a drawer and came out with gold coins. He rose and walked around the desk, cash in hand. "Let me thank you for the services rendered to the Butterfield Stage Company."

Calhoun took the money and shook Ferguson's hand. Then he counted the money as Ferguson went back to his seat. "Those two have been a thorn in the company's side for months, Mister Calhoun, and I, for one, am damn glad to be rid of them."

Calhoun nodded, figuring there was no need to say anything.

"How was the journey otherwise?" Ferguson asked.

"No troubles," Osgood said. "I thought we were gonna have some with Mrs. McGowan, there for a while, though."

"Oh?"

"Two passengers were crowdin' her some. Joel spoke to them a few times when she complained, but they denied doing anything wrong. Besides, Joel couldn't spend his time in the coach, so he wasn't sure what exactly was goin' on. After we offered Mister Calhoun a ride for helpin' us, we heard of no more trouble."

"Talked to those two, did you, Mister Calhoun?" Ferguson asked with a smile of appreciation that someone stood up for standards these days.

Calhoun nodded. "I never could abide women bein' favored with unwanted attention."

"There's too few men in this world who feel that way, Mister Calhoun," Ferguson said. "Most are too willing to look the other way when such things occur. It's a shame that womanhood has to put up with such things." He paused. "Well, then, Frank, Joel, I expect you boys're tired after your long journey. Go on and eat and take your leisure while it lasts. Mister Calhoun, I'd be obliged if you were to stay here for a few minutes."

Calhoun shrugged and nodded. As the two stage employees left the room, Calhoun stood and poured himself another decent shot of whiskey, then sat again.

When they were alone, Ferguson said, "Let me apologize again for my behavior before, Mister Calhoun. It was uncalled for. The only excuse I can offer is that my mind is occupied with troubles the company is facing. That's also why I asked you to stay a little." He sighed. "Have you any plans, Mister Calhoun?"

Calhoun shook his head.

"You have nowhere you need to be?"

Another shake of the head.

"I know you have at least a hundred and fifty dollars on you now," Ferguson said with a smile. "A not inconsiderable sum, of course, but not nearly enough to last you at leisure for a while."

"True," Calhoun acknowledged. "Now get to the point."

Ferguson nodded. "Do you need a job, Mister Calhoun?"

"Can't say as I *need* one," Calhoun allowed. "Don't mean I won't take one if the right one was to come along."

"I have one in mind that might be just right for you." He paused a moment, collecting his thoughts. He had just made his decision to do this minutes ago, and he was still not quite sure how to phrase it. He decided to just plunge ahead.

"I suppose that you've figured out that the robbery you stopped was not an isolated event." When Calhoun nodded, Ferguson went on. "And that's not the least of the troubles we have with robbers. Our stages don't carry too much in the way of valuables, since this line, or at least this section of the line, is not near any gold fields. About all we carry that has any worth is the mail. And whatever the passengers have on them."

"You still ain't made your point," Calhoun interjected.

"I'm getting there, Mister Calhoun. Bear with me a little. While robberies like that one are common enough along this stretch of the Butterfield line, the much larger problem is horse thieves."

"Horse thieves?"

"Horse thieves," Ferguson said with a nod. "The bastards've hit every Butterfield station between Fort Smith and Fort Belknap at least once, I believe, except Fort Smith, Cross River, and Fort Belknap. The problem is larger between here and Fort Belknap. I expect they're selling—or more probably trading—the company horses and mules they run off."

"And you want me to do something about the problem?"

Ferguson nodded. "Yes, I do, Mister Calhoun. Find the bastards and bring them to heel. I don't give a good goddamn if you catch them and put them in jail or if you kill them all."

"You know who's doin' it?" Calhoun asked as he finished off the small glass of whiskey. With somewhere around eighty dollars left of the money he had won off Claude Hopkins and the hundred fifty Ferguson had just given him, he was set up well enough for a while. He was not one who worried overly much about money, and even if he bought a horse, he'd be all right. Still, he had always figured it worthwhile to listen to job offers, just in case.

"Not for certain," Ferguson admitted. "But I'm damn near sure Indians're doing it."

"Indians you say?" Calhoun countered, interest piqued.

"Yes, Mister Calhoun, Indians. I find it hard to believe that the Chickasaws might be doing it, since we're on good terms with them, as well as the Choctaws, who're more populous in these parts. But the Comanches, now that's another thing entirely."

"You still have Comanches runnin' around here?" Calhoun was a little surprised.

"No. Not regularly. They were driven out of this region some years back, I suppose. Still, the Comanches are Indians who think nothing of riding hundreds of miles to raid, especially if there're prime horses to be had. They can drive them to the Llano and trade them to the Comancheros for whiskey and guns with which they can wreak more havoc among the citizens hereabout. Or they can trade them to the damn Mexicans below the border. Those goddamn greasers're willing to do anything to get back at us after we won that war against them." He paused. "I suspect, too, that they're trading or selling them to the Choctaws. Even though we get along with those Indians, they're still Indians, if you know what I mean."

Calhoun nodded. There was nothing to say, since Ferguson's comments were true. Instead, he asked, "What're you offerin'?"

"Well," Ferguson said, leaning back again. This might be a touchy area, and he wanted to present a demeanor of calmness and certainty. "I wasn't figuring on paying a salary," he said smoothly. "If I did that, you or anyone else might take advantage, and draw this out over months just to keep the money coming in. What I'm prepared to do, though, is to offer you a horse; a mule for packing supplies, if you want; all your supplies; and free lodging in any Butterfield way station or in a town the stage runs through."

"No money at all?" Calhoun asked. He couldn't believe Ferguson would try to pull such a thing.

"Of course there'll be money. If you're any good," Ferguson said pointedly. "You'll get any and all reward money on any of the thieves you get. Dead or alive."

"No, thanks," Calhoun said, setting the glass on the desk and rising.

"Why not?" Ferguson asked, surprised.

"How many places offer rewards on Indians? If you think Comanches or any other goddamn redskins are behind this, there ain't gonna be any reward money."

Ferguson nodded. "I never thought about that," he admitted. "Wait, sit, please." He thought a while. "I'll have to trust you this way, but I'll give you a hundred dollars a head for any Comanche you bring in that's stealin' horses from us. Since all Comanches steal horses, they're all horse thieves. I'd hope, though, that you'd concentrate on the ones stealing company horses and mules. You can also have any reward offered on any white bandits like those two you took care of the other day. How's that sound?"

"It's a deal, Mister Ferguson," Calhoun said. It was just the kind of job he was used to—and good at. With his skills at tracking and in using firearms, he was well-suited to such work. It also would keep him off on his own most of the time, something he always considered a benefit. But most of all, it would allow him to hunt down Indians, in whose blood he someday hoped to quench the fires of hatred and loss that burned in his chest.

CHAPTER

* 8 *

Irene McGowan was rather pleased—or so Calhoun liked to think—to see Calhoun when he showed up at her boardinghouse and quietly asked for a room.

"For how long?" she asked, a bit flustered at being in his presence again.

Calhoun shrugged. "The stage company hired me to do some work for them," he said. "Most of it'll be out on the trail, but there'll be times I'll be back here and will need a place to stay."

"I can keep your room for you," Irene said shyly.

"I'd be obliged."

"You want a room downstairs?"

"Second floor, if you have one."

Irene nodded. "Follow me." She headed up the stairs, her heart beating fast. She stopped at a room and opened the door. "My room's next door," she said, face flushed.

Calhoun nodded and walked inside. He saw no reason to say anything and increase her embarrassment. It was obvious that she was interested in him, and he knew he would do something about that sooner or later. But he could wait until she was a little more used to the idea.

Irene followed him into the room, but left the door open. "Supper's at six each night, Mister Calhoun."

"Wade."

"All right . . . Wade." She hesitated, still as nervous as a steer in a thunderstorm. "Breakfast is at six, too. Both meals're included in your rent."

"Thank you, ma'am."

"Please, Wade, call me Irene," she said softly.

He nodded and dropped his saddle in a corner, glad to be relieved of its weight. He surveyed the room. It was stark, with only a bed, nightstand, small chest of drawers, two lanterns, one on the wall, and a basin and water pitcher. Sun streamed in from the single window. Calhoun pulled a double eagle from his pocket and held it out to Irene.

"I can't take that, Mister . . . Wade," she said in protest. "It's too much."

"I got enough. Take it. When I use that up, tell me."

Irene McGowan had used all of her savings for the trip back east, and twenty dollars looked pretty good to her right now. While her boarders had been paying their rent while she was gone, she was low on household supplies and any extra money would be a blessing. She tentatively took the coin and dropped it into the pocket of her calico dress. She had changed as soon as she had gotten back, swapping her only fancy dress, which she had wanted for traveling so she would look presentable. She now wore a plain calico, with a high, button-front bodice and long sleeves.

"Well, ma'am," Calhoun finally said, "I'd best get cleaned up some for supper."

Irene nodded. "Then you'll be joining us?"

"Yep." When Irene left, Calhoun scraped the several days' growth of beard off his face, and washed up a little.

Then he went and stood looking out the window, puffing on a cigarette, feeling the window-glass-warmed sun beating on his face and chest.

Soon after, Irene knocked on his door and called, "Supper's on, Mister Calhoun."

He opened the window and flicked his second cigarette through it, watching as it swirled down to the street below. Leaving the window open, he headed downstairs.

Irene's boarders were about what he expected—a collection of unmarried working men and travelers stopping in Cross River for a few days or weeks. For the most part, they were more interested in filling their stomachs than they were in talking, which suited Calhoun. Each of the boarders had looked at Calhoun, seen the hard, pocked face and deadly blue eyes and decided that he was not interested in chattering.

Only one of them was of any note to Calhoun. He was a young man, fairly tall, with a slim, open face, and lively eyes under a shock of unruly brown hair. The only reason Calhoun really noticed him was because the man's eyes were almost constantly on Irene.

Calhoun also took note of the fact that Irene paid no more attention to the man than she did any of the others, except Calhoun. She made sure he had good portions of the best food she had, kept his coffee cup filled, and was in other ways highly solicitous of him. Calhoun did not mind the attention.

Calhoun was up early for breakfast and to watch the stage pull out, again heading south. He noted that the gambler and the bunko artist were on it. Had they not been, Calhoun figured he would've have to kill one or both of them sooner or later because they surely would've tried something with Irene as soon as he left town.

Frank Osgood strolled up to where he was standing and watched with him. After the stage had left, Calhoun said, "How come you and Joel have to cross the Red all the time?"

"It's where the town is," Osgood said, brow wrinkled in puzzlement.

"But why on this side of the river? Why not on the other side?"

"Oh," Osgood said, finally understanding. "Mainly, I think, because that's Indian land over there. By putting the stage office on this side of the river, knowing a town would grow up around it, the company figured it'd have a lot less trouble over land ownership and all."

"Makes sense," Calhoun agreed. "Well, Frank, I've got things to do." Calhoun left to take care of the mundane chores necessary to get ready for his new job. The main chore was finding a horse. It was when he was looking some animals over that the irony of his new work hit him: he, a man whose poor luck with horses approached the legendary, was to run down a band of horse thieves. Had he been a man with a sense of humor, he would've laughed himself nearly sick at it.

Still, finding a horse was not easy. For him it never was. He finally settled on a motley-looking, light bay mare that had a black tail and black mane. The stable owner swore that though the horse didn't look all that good, it was a sturdy and dependable mount.

Calhoun opted not to take a mule with supplies. He simply took enough food to last several days and asked for and got a letter from Henry Ferguson that would introduce him to station managers along the way. With that, he would be able to get food or shelter along the stage road, without having to care for a mule.

When he went to Ferguson to get the letter that afternoon, Ferguson filled him in a little more on the job he faced.

"You'll range an area of a hundred fifty, maybe two hundred miles. From the Choctaw town of Kiamichi up near the Ouachita Mountains to Sharp Bend on the Brazos River."

"Hell of an area," Calhoun commented after a swallow of whiskey.

"That it is. We can narrow it down some, though. Most of the horse thieving has been taking place between here and the way station on Denton Creek. The robberies of the stages have been mainly up in Indian country."

Calhoun nodded. It made sense, in a way. White robbers would feel more comfortable in holding up stages in Indian country, since Arkansas and Texas would be reluctant to send lawmen in there. By the same token, Indians, especially Comanches, would be more interested in stealing horses from whites than from other Indians, especially since the white settlements were closer. "Where'd the last robbery take place?"

"You know that as well as I do," Ferguson said with a humorless smile. "But to tell you the truth, Mister Calhoun, I'm a lot more interested in catching the horse thieves than I am in the highwaymen."

"Oh?" Calhoun asked, surprised.

"The highwaymen haven't killed anyone," Ferguson explained. "The most they do is rob the mail and relieve the passengers of their valuables. Certainly nothing I—or the company—condone, of course, but right now the least of our worries. The horse thieving, though, is costing the company a fortune, Mister Calhoun. We've lost nearly two hundred prime horses and fifty or sixty mules in the past few months. That's what I want stopped. If you find any highwaymen in the process, take them."

Calhoun nodded. "All right. Then where were the last horses taken from?"

"A station down on Clear Creek. Will Templeton's the station master. You planning to start there?"

Calhoun nodded again. "I'll leave first thing tomorrow."

"You have everything you need? A horse? Mule? Supplies?"

"No mule. Got everything else I need." He rose. "The letter?"

"Yes, of course," Ferguson said. "I almost forgot." He quickly scratched it out, blotted it and handed it to Calhoun. "Good luck, Mister Calhoun."

Calhoun shrugged. He never trusted to luck. He simply trusted to himself and to his survival instincts, though he cursed the latter more often than not. They had kept him alive through many a time where he wished he had died, so that he could be with his Lizbeth and Lottie again. But he had never had any luck in that either.

Calhoun went back to his room at the boardinghouse and got ready to leave the next day. He cleaned and reloaded all his weapons, figuring it better to waste some powder and ball now than to worry about a misfire when he needed the guns. Then he repacked his saddlebags with his new supplies. He opened his bedroll and hung it half out the window to air, and then sharpened his bowie knife.

By the time he was finished, it was almost time for

supper. He rolled his bedroll back up and then smoked down a cigarette, until Irene called him for supper.

Once again he noted that the young man would not—or maybe could not—take his eyes off Irene. It meant little to him, other than the fact that he wondered how the man would take the disappointment of finding that Irene wanted nothing to do with him.

After eating, Calhoun headed out and wandered to the Red River saloon, where he spent a few hours sipping rye whiskey, playing a little stud poker, and just watching the comings and goings of the people of Cross River. They really held no interest for him, but he had learned over the years to be wary, and keeping an eye on the people around him was the best way to do that.

Finally he wandered through the lantern-lit streets back to the boardinghouse. Irene was in the sitting room just off the foyer, and she called out to him. When he stepped inside the room, he spotted the moon-eyed young man.

"Please sit a spell, Mister Calhoun," she said, a note of pleading in her voice.

"You sure, ma'am?" he countered, wanting to make sure.

"Yes." Her eyes reinforced the word.

Calhoun's eyes flicked to the young man and then back to Irene.

"Oh, forgive me," Irene said. "I've lost my manners. Mister Wade Calhoun, Mister Alvin Webb."

Calhoun nodded at Webb, who scowled, but then said, "Howdy." The sentiment was not warm.

Calhoun sat and rolled a cigarette.

"Some coffee, Mister Calhoun?" Irene asked.

"Don't mind if I do." He was not above sitting here

and annoying Webb, especially if it helped to endear him to Irene a little.

When he had his coffee, Calhoun sipped at it while smoking his cigarette. He, Webb, and Irene were silent. Calhoun didn't mind; indeed, he preferred it that way. It was also somewhat humorous to see Webb sitting there fuming.

Finally, after perhaps half an hour, Irene stood. "Would you please escort me to my room, Mister Calhoun?" she asked in a firm voice.

"Yes'm." He stood.

"Good night, Mister Webb," Irene said with something approaching finality in her voice. She slid her hand through the crook in Calhoun's left arm and walked with him into the hallway and up the stairs.

When they stopped in front of Irene's door, she turned and placed her hands lightly on Calhoun's forearms. "Thank you, Wade," she said in relief. "I'm afraid Mister Webb is rather attracted to me. . . ."

"Can't blame any man for that," Calhoun said honestly.

Irene smiled. "Trouble is, though, he won't let me alone."

"Don't you like him?"

"Oh, I guess I like him a little. He's a nice young man. But he's . . . he's not what I want, I guess you could say. I'm not attracted to him in that . . . way . . . You know what I mean." She flushed.

Calhoun nodded. "Yes, I know. Want me to talk to him? Tell him to leave you alone?"

"Could you? I . . . I really hate to impose on you, what with all you've done for me already. But Mister Webb makes me uncomfortable. Unlike you." She gasped when she had actually voiced the latter.

"You go on in now, Irene. I'll talk to Webb before I leave."

"You're going tomorrow?"

Calhoun nodded. "First light. I've got a heap of travelin' to do."

"I'll miss you," Irene said before she fled into her room and shut the door behind her.

Shaking his head a little, Calhoun walked back downstairs. Webb was just coming out of the sitting room. He turned a glowering face on Calhoun, and tried to push past him. Calhoun would not budge, and said, "A word with you, Mister Webb."

"I got nothin' to say to you, boy," Webb snapped.

"I got somethin' to say to you." He grabbed Webb's arm, turned him and shoved him toward the sitting room.

Inside, Webb turned, face twisted in fury. He was about to say something, but Calhoun held a finger to his lips. "This's no time to be makin' a lot of noise," Calhoun warned. "You say the wrong thing to me, and I'll knock you on your ass."

"What do you want?" Webb asked tightly.

"Miss Irene asked me to tell you to leave her alone," Calhoun said evenly.

"Hogwash," Webb snorted. "You just want to court her yourself, so you're tellin' me this story."

"Let me tell you somethin', boy," Calhoun said harshly. "If I wanted to court Irene and you were in the way, you'd be dead now. I'm just tellin' you her wishes."

"I don't believe you."

Calhoun shrugged. "It don't matter. You bother her again and you'll get hurt." He turned and strolled away.

CHAPTER

* 9 *

The station at Clear Creek was about what Calhoun had expected. A good-sized, tilted building of mud, sod, and logs; a similarly constructed, though larger, barn; and a rickety corral of sagging logs between the two. Calhoun counted almost two dozen horses and six mules in the corral. From where he sat on a small ridge a quarter of a mile away, he could see someone working in the "yard" in front of the station.

Clear Creek ran sluggishly behind the station. It was narrow, muddy and, Calhoun figured, not very deep. Still, it would provide fresh water for the animals, as well as the travelers, and during the summers that would be important.

Calhoun rolled a cigarette and sat there on his new bay horse, just looking over the landscape. He noticed after a bit that the man working outside the station had spotted him and had stood there for a minute or so gazing up at the ridge. Then the man turned and headed inside the station house.

Calhoun stamped the cigarette butt out on his left palm and then rode down toward the station. He was still ten yards away when a rifle barrel poked out a slit in the wood shutter over one window.

"That's close enough, mister," a gruff voice said from inside.

Calhoun stopped, eyes narrowed.

"What's your business here?" the voice asked from inside.

"You Templeton?" Calhoun countered.

"I might be. Who wants to know?"

"Name's Wade Calhoun. Henry Ferguson sent me to . . ."

"Bullshit. Now ride on out. You can go any direction you want, so long as it's away from here."

"Ferguson ain't gonna be happy with this."

"I'll worry about that another time, mister. Now beat the dust."

Calhoun sat only a moment, then shrugged and moved off, heading around the building. He was aware more by instinct than anything else, that a rifle—maybe the same, maybe someone else with one—followed him as he splashed across the little creek. He had been right in his figuring, in that the creek was not very deep.

He rode a mile or a little more, then turned north. He rode slowly, until he came to Clear Creek again a couple miles northwest of the station. He found a small grove of trees with a thicket winding through it, and he pulled in. He unsaddled the bay, tended it, gathered firewood, and started a fire. After cooking and eating a simple meal of bacon and beans—which he was almost out of now—he stretched out on his bedroll, head against a small log, and fell asleep.

Calhoun awoke just before dark. He ate again, had two cups of coffee and a cigarette, and then saddled his horse. He crossed the creek and then followed it southeastward toward the station. It was night now, but the moon and plenty of stars provided sufficient light to see some distance.

When he spotted the bulky shadow of the station, Calhoun stopped and dismounted. He tied his reins to the cannon of the horse's left foreleg so the animal couldn't move too easily. Then he marched forward, thankful that the light breeze was blowing into his face.

He was almost at the house before a dog started barking inside. Calhoun swiftly slid along the front wall of the building until he was right next to the door.

Light suddenly spilled out into the yard as the door opened. The same gruff voice as before growled, "Shut up, Rex." Then a man came out, rifle in his hands.

Calhoun reached out, latched his hands onto the gun barrel and yanked. Calhoun used the momentum to swing the man around and slam him up against the wall of the station. Calhoun jerked the rifle free and threw it away. He slammed a punch into the man's midsection. "You Templeton?" he asked, voice harsh and flat.

Before the man could answer, someone pasted Calhoun a good shot on the side of the head. Calhoun groaned, and as he fell, he figured he had been hit by a pistol barrel.

He had no time to wonder about it, though, as a small but viciously growling dog suddenly jumped on him, fangs heading for his throat. Calhoun managed to get his left arm up and jam his forearm crossways into the dog's mouth. He grabbed the dog by the neck. The dog bucked and jumped, but Calhoun kept his desperate grip on the animal, and struggled up at the same time.

Calhoun slammed the dog into the man who had first come out of the house. The man fell and the dog yelped. Calhoun and the animal let go of each other at the same time.

Calhoun spun and saw a blocky, young man bringing a pistol up toward him. Calhoun was on the verge of just drawing his own revolver and drilling the man, but he decided they wasn't necessary right now. He charged instead, tackling the man and then pounding him.

Calhoun heard the snarling of the dog heading in his direction, and he suddenly rolled to the side. As the dog skidded on the dirt in trying to stop, Calhoun swung his legs around and booted the animal in the side. The dog yapped and ran off, heading into the house.

Calhoun got up, kicked away the young man's pistol, and headed for the other man, who had gotten up and was looking for his rifle. Calhoun plowed into him and rammed him against the wall. He hammered the man three times, twice in the stomach and once in the face, before swinging him around and shoving him.

The man stumbled and crashed into the younger man, who had finally gotten up again. Both fell.

Calhoun was breathing hard and had had his fill of these two oafs. He jerked out a Dragoon, cocked it and aimed it at the two men. "Is one of you Will Templeton?" he asked, voice hard.

The older man, who was wheezing a little, nodded and choked out, "Me."

"What in hell was this all about?" Calhoun asked.

"Thought you were a horse thief."

"I told you Henry Ferguson sent me. I'm here to catch the damn horse thieves."

"We didn't know."

"Shit," Calhoun muttered. "Come here," he ordered.

Templeton edged up, holding his stomach.

With his left hand, Calhoun reached into his pocket and pulled out the letter from Ferguson. He handed it to Templeton. "Read it."

Templeton glanced at Calhoun, then took the paper and opened it. "I need some light," he said warily.

Calhoun nodded. As Templeton shuffled backward toward the door, Calhoun followed, keeping close. He also made sure that the younger man did not move. "Far enough," Calhoun finally said.

Templeton read the letter, then looked up at Calhoun. "You should've shown me this before," he said in an accusatory tone.

"Jesus," Calhoun muttered, annoyed all over again.

"Guess I never give you a chance, huh?" Templeton said.

"Nope." Calhoun paused. "You believe me now?"

Templeton nodded. "Sorry, Mister . . ." he glanced at the paper again ". . . Mister Calhoun. I'll give you all the help I can."

Calhoun nodded. He waved the pistol at the younger man. "Who's he?"

"My son, Dewey."

"The letter?" Calhoun said, holding out his hand.

Templeton handed the paper back and Calhoun folded it one handed and shoved it back into his pocket. Then he put his pistol away. "Either of you crosses me again and I'll kill you," he warned. "Now, let's go inside."

"Our guns?" Templeton asked. "We ain't had trouble in a couple of weeks, but you never know when it's going to happen. That's why I was mistrustful of you before."

Calhoun nodded. The thought was reasonable. "You find 'em," he said, pointing to Dewey. "One at a time and bring 'em to me."

Dewey found his pistol first and gave it to Calhoun, who pulled the caps off and dropped them in the dirt. When Dewey brought the rifle, Calhoun handed him the pistol back. He unloaded the rifle and gave it to Templeton. "All right, inside," Calhoun said.

Calhoun followed the two men into the house. The station was divided into several rooms. The major room was the one they were in. It encompassed the kitchen, a large dining area with two long tables with a bench on each side, and a large sleeping area with rickety cots on which rested lice-filled ticking mattresses. The other rooms, Calhoun assumed, were sleeping quarters for the Templetons.

"My wife, Elva," Templeton said, indicating a tall, spindly, once-attractive woman standing by the stove. Her face was etched with weariness from too harsh a life.

"Ma'am," Calhoun said. He noted that the dog lay cowering in a corner.

"Are you hungry, mister?" Elva asked.

Calhoun shook his head. "I could use some coffee, though," he volunteered.

Templeton hung his rifle on two pegs over the front door. Dewey put the pistol into a holster hanging from a wood peg beside the door.

"Sit, Mister Calhoun," Templeton said. He walked to a box resting in a corner near the stove and fished out a bottle of whiskey. When his wife had poured coffee for him and Calhoun, Templeton added a good dollop of whiskey to the two coffee cups. "It ain't the best sippin' whiskey a man could have," he apologized, "but it's a far sight better'n none a'tall. Drink up, Mister Calhoun."

Calhoun was almost as annoyed with Templeton's sudden attempts to be friendly as he had been when he was attacked by Templeton. But he said nothing. He figured that Templeton was just trying to make up for the poor welcome he had given Calhoun. He sipped, and couldn't decide which was more foul, the whiskey or the coffee. Both were among the worst he had ever had. He managed to keep the grimace off his face, though.

Dewey took some coffee from his mother and added whiskey. Then he sat next to his father.

It gave Calhoun his first real good look at the Templeton men. Templeton himself was about forty-five with a powerful-looking body and big stomach. His face was creased from wind and weather, and burned darkly from exposure. His hands were oversized and full of cuts and cracks. He looked to be a man who could handle the harsh demands of existing in a place like this.

His son was maybe twenty or twenty-five and slightly smaller than Templeton. He showed none of the ravages of time and hard living that his father had acquired, but Calhoun figured he would before too many more years had passed. He wondered what a big, strapping, healthy young man like Dewey Templeton did for female companionship out here in the middle of nowhere. He wouldn't put it past the younger Templeton—or the older one, for that matter—to abase women travelers on the stage.

"When were the horse thieves through here last?" Calhoun finally asked.

"Two, two and a half weeks ago," Templeton said, squinting as he tried to remember. "It was the third time in the past six months. That's why I was some suspicious of you when you come along."

"You had given me a chance to show you Ferguson's letter, we could've avoided all this trouble."

Templeton nodded. "I know that now. But, hell, I look up, and see a rider—someone I ain't ever seen before—sitting on his horse up on that ridge lookin' this place over. After all the troubles we've had, what the hell was I suppose to think?" He sounded defensive.

Calhoun shrugged. "Ferguson thinks the horse thieves're Indians. Probably Comanches. I ain't Indian," he said flatly.

"Ferguson tell you that?"

Calhoun nodded. "Ain't that true?"

"I ain't so sure." Templeton drank some more coffee and watched as his wife went to a chair and picked up some sewing. "It's the likeliest thing, I suppose, but I ain't ever caught no Indians at it." He smiled with regret. "I ain't caught any white men at it either."

"Which means it's probably Indians," Dewey said, "the sneaky, red bastards."

"Watch your tongue, boy," Elva said quietly from her chair.

"Yes'm," Dewey answered sheepishly.

"Your son's probably right," Calhoun said. He drained the fetid liquid in his cup, fighting back a grimace, and then set the cup down. "You follow 'em any of those times?"

"No, sirree," Templeton said emphatically. "I can be a tough customer when the need arises, Mister Calhoun, but I ain't tanglin' with a bunch of horse thieves, red or white, but especially red."

"You see any signs at all of which way they went?"

"Looks like they headed north from what I could see."

"North?" Calhoun was surprised. "If it was Comanches, they would've headed west most likely."

"True enough. But just 'cause they started out north don't mean they kept goin' that way. Or if they did keep goin' that way, they might've had a reason."

"Such as?" Calhoun prompted.

"Such as sellin' 'em to the Cherokees or the Choctaws or one of those other goddamn tribes up there. Or they could've been headin' for Kansas Territory to Kiowa country. The Comanches and the Kiowas're real friendly, and it ain't unknown for some of one tribe to raid with some of the other."

Calhoun nodded. That all made sense. "Anything else you can tell me about the thieves?" he asked.

Templeton shook his head. "Nope. I just hope you can catch the bastards before they do any more raidin'. And I'll tell you this: I don't envy you your task in the least, Mister Calhoun. To speak bluntly, I think you made a damn fool decision in takin' on this particular job." He smiled a little to let Calhoun know he was not insulting Calhoun, just commenting on the situation.

"You could be right, Mister Templeton," Calhoun said. "You mind if I stay the night here?"

"'Course not," Templeton said.

"You two and the dog gonna leave me be?"

"Yessir," Templeton said without hesitation. Suddenly he got a puzzled look on his face. "Where's your horse, Mister Calhoun?" he asked.

"Left back out there a little ways. Northwest, I suspect." He stood. "I best go get him."

"Set and relax, Mister Calhoun," Templeton said. "Dewey'll take care of your horse for you."

CHAPTER

* 10 *

Calhoun spent several days riding due north, glad to be away from Will Templeton and his son. And glad to be eating his own food again. That shocked him, since he had always hated eating his own cooking. But the slop Elva Templeton had fed him was inedible. At least to him. He found out that the Templetons' dog, Rex, didn't mind it, and he had made friends with the dog as he fed the animal bits of food from the plate of swill Elva had put in front of him. The dog seemed to forgive him for kicking him in the fight the night before.

When he reached the Red River, he swam his horse across the river and angled northeast. There was no trail of the horse thieves for even an expert tracker like him to follow, not after a few weeks and at least one rainstorm. He mainly just followed his instincts, hoping he came across something that would help him.

He saw nothing of interest or help for some days, and he was about to turn back toward Cross River, when he spotted what appeared to be a town—or maybe just a settlement—along the Clear Boggy River. That surprised him, and so he stopped to roll a cigarette and mull it over a bit. There were not supposed to be any white settlements out here, though that's what this appeared to be.

Log houses chinked with mud were scattered around a few "streets" amid the trees. Fields were cleared, and the new season's planting of corn, potatoes, peas, pumpkins, beans, and melons was already sprouting. Other fields were planted with cotton. Calhoun spotted several slaves working in the fields. He could see fenced-in corrals with hogs, cattle, and horses. He spotted a church, what he thought to be a school, a cotton gin, and, farther down the river, what appeared to be a salt works.

He finally flipped the cigarette butt into the water and then rode across the creek, heading for the nearest log house he had seen. There was little activity, and he was almost to the first house when he saw one of the residents in the corral, and he pulled up sharply.

"Goddamn," he muttered to himself. He had heard of Indians in these parts who were living—or trying to live—like white men, but he had never really believed it. But that was an Indian sure as anything there in the corral, spreading hay around for a small herd of horses. Calhoun had no doubt about it, despite the fact that the man was wearing white man's clothes.

Calhoun shrugged and rode on. He might as well stop and ask questions here as ride on. There was always a chance he could learn something. He stopped at the corral and dismounted, pausing to stretch his legs.

The Indian looked at him in curiosity, then went back to what he was doing.

Calhoun leaned on the top log rail of the corral fence and put one foot on the bottom one, watching the Indian, whom he figured to be a Choctaw, based on the area he was in more than anything else. The Indian was of medium height and well built, with a lithe, muscular way of moving. His hair was fairly short, but raven black, and his skin was quite dark.

The Choctaw finally finished spreading the hay, then ambled to where Calhoun leaned against the fence. "Somethin' I can do for you?" the Indian drawled.

"I'm interested in some horses," Calhoun said, bending the truth just a tad. He noted the man's intense, very dark eyes, and the wisp of a mustache.

"I ain't got many, and I ain't of a mood to sell what I got," the Choctaw said.

"What's your name?" Calhoun asked tightly.

"George Franklin," the Indian answered in kind. "Yours?"

"Wade Calhoun."

"Please to make your acquaintance, Mister Calhoun. Now get the hell off my land."

It took some moments for Calhoun to bat down the anger that had flared inside him, though someone looking at him couldn't tell he was angry. "I'm willin' to pay well for the horses," he lied evenly. "Mind if I take a look?"

Franklin shrugged. "Look all you want. I ain't gonna sell."

Calhoun glowered at Franklin a moment before climbing through the fence. He took a look at two of the seven horses. Both had the Butterfield brand on them. Calhoun suspected several of the others did, too. He turned and walked over to Franklin, who was leaning back against the fence, elbows hooked over one of the rails.

"Where'd you get them two horses, Mister Franklin?" he asked harshly.

Franklin spit into the dirt, dark face scowling. "None of your damn business."

"I can make it my business."

Franklin shrugged. "You gonna shoot me?" he asked. "Shit. Your people've been rubbin' my ass the wrong way as long as I can remember. You can't do nothin' to me."

Calhoun accepted that. He still hated Franklin, simply because he was an Indian. His poor attitude didn't help matters, but Calhoun didn't have to like the Choctaw to accept his statement as fact. "You don't have to protect the Comanches, you know," Calhoun said. He rolled a cigarette.

"What'n the hell're you talkin' about, mister?" Franklin asked, surprised.

Calhoun was about to stick the cigarette in his mouth and light it, but he suddenly held it out. "Smoke?" he asked. He figured there was no harm in maybe trying to be a little friendly here. It might help him get some answers more easily.

Franklin took the cigarette and fired it up while Calhoun rolled another.

"I'm trackin' some horse thieves," Calhoun said through a cloud of cigarette smoke. "I figure the Comanches're the thieves. I also think they're bringin' the stolen horses up here and sellin' 'em to you and your people."

"That's the goddamnedest most stupid thing I ever heard," Franklin said with a snort.

Calhoun battled down the anger again. "Two of the horses you got in here're stolen. They still got the Butterfield brand on 'em."

"They got the Butterfield brand all right, but only 'cause I ain't had time to put my own brand on 'em.

And I don't know nothin' about no stolen horses. I bought them damn animals."

"I don't suppose you got a bill of sale?" Calhoun asked sarcastically.

"I sure do," Franklin said, staring passively at Calhoun.

"Comanches don't give no bills of sale."

"I didn't get it from no Comanches. I got it from one of your people."

"A white man?" Calhoun asked, somewhat incredulous.

Franklin nodded.

"Bullshit. Let me see that bill of sale."

"No," Franklin said flatly.

Calhoun had had about enough of this uncooperative Choctaw. He dropped his cigarette and launched a punch at Franklin.

The Choctaw darted his head out of the way, and Calhoun's fist hit nothing but air. Franklin then pounded Calhoun a good shot in the ribs.

Calhoun grunted, more surprised than hurt, though the punch had not been a light one. He saw red, too, enraged that this Indian would make him look like a fool. He had little time for thought, though, as Franklin charged at him. The two tumbled down in the dusty, hay-covered corral, and wrestled on the ground, each trying to gain some kind of edge. Calhoun began to think that he had somehow gotten ahold of a cougar. The Choctaw was a mass of muscle, speed, and agility, and it was all he could do to keep Franklin from taking advantage and doing him some serious damage.

They rolled into the legs of a horse, which nickered nervously. All the animals shuffled, trying to get away from this strange thing crawling around on the ground making odd noises.

Calhoun suddenly became aware of being hauled to his feet. It wasn't Franklin doing it. Then he saw that others were pulling Franklin up.

When the two combatants were standing, an old man with long gray hair and dark, impassive face, asked, "What's going on here?" His voice was a little slurred, as if he had too much saliva flowing.

"That son of a bitch called me a horse thief," Franklin said flatly.

"Why?" the old man asked.

"Who're you?" Calhoun asked, jerking his arms free of the Choctaw men who held him.

The gray-haired Indian said something that to Calhoun sounded like a combination of a pig's snuffling and a human's grunt.

Calhoun looked at the Choctaw in bewilderment. "Means damn fool, does it?" he asked cockily.

The Indian scowled. "You can call me Jackson. Sam Jackson."

"That doesn't tell me who you are."

"I'm the leader of this band of Choctaws. Among your people, I'd be something of a mixture of mayor and sheriff."

Calhoun nodded. "I'm Wade Calhoun. Mister Ferguson of the Butterfield company hired me to find who was stealin' the company's horses."

"So you just came up here and blamed the first Indian you found?" Jackson asked harshly.

Calhoun shook his head. "The company thinks Comanches're doin' it. The last time horses were stolen, they headed up this way. I found at least two Butterfield horses in Franklin's corral here. I asked how he got 'em, figurin' the Comanches come up here and sold 'em to him."

"And what did George tell you?" Jackson questioned.

"That a white man sold 'em to him."

"But you don't believe that?"

Calhoun shook his head.

"Why?" Jackson asked. "Is it easier for you to believe an Indian—any Indian—did it, than to believe his word?"

Jackson had hit the nail on the head, Calhoun admitted silently, but he was not about to acknowledge that to these Choctaws. He just shrugged.

"Would my word be any more acceptable than George's?" Jackson asked.

Calhoun shook his head.

"I figured." Jackson sighed. "I'll tell you anyway, Mister Calhoun," he said patiently. "The ones stealin' Butterfield horses are white men. Sometimes they come up here and we buy some of those horses. They're a lot cheaper'n than if we go to Cross River or Fort Smith or anyplace else."

"I thought you were friends of the Butterfield company."

"We are," Franklin said with a shrug. "But my people learned a long time ago, Mister Calhoun, that we must look out for ourselves. We trade the horses or sell them to the army or even to the stage line, usually through another party. We make some money, and your people get some of their horses back. You see, Mister Calhoun, none of you people'll believe us when we tell 'em white men're stealin' the horses."

"You know any of 'em?" Calhoun asked despite himself.

"The leader's a man named Micah Alexander."

"Why didn't you tell anybody this?"

"You ain't the only one don't believe Indians," Jackson said sourly. "Ain't no one gonna believe an Indian who says somethin' against a white man, no matter how bad that white man is."

Calhoun wasn't sure if he should believe him. What Jackson had said was true, but on the other hand, the Choctaw could just be spouting off. "I expect that's true," he allowed.

"Now, if you was maybe a federal marshal," Jackson said. "Or even a county sheriff from south of the Red, we might be a little more open to helpin' you. But seein' that you ain't jack shit, you've got about all the information you're gonna get here. I suggest you climb on your horse and ride out of Choctaw land, Mister Calhoun. Or I'll let them loose on you," he added, pointing to his men.

"I can take a hint," Calhoun said agreeably, though he was seething inside again. "You may be seein' me again, Chief," he said, a little sarcastically.

"Then our next meetin' might not be so friendly," Jackson said flatly.

"That might be interestin'" Calhoun rolled a cigarette, his moves slow and deliberate. He lit it and then walked off, heading toward the downed rails of the corral. He walked through and untied his horse. Without looking back, he rode out of the Choctaw village.

He made his way through the settlement under the dark, wary eyes of the Choctaws. Even the children peered out from behind door jambs or buildings, watching him rather fearfully. Seeing the frightened looks on the faces of the women and children made Calhoun think. When he did, he was convinced that the

Choctaws were lying to him about the horse thefts. Trouble was, there was little or nothing he could do about it right now.

He rode north, and then east, angling to where he would cut the stage road. There was no reason for it; it just seemed a reasonable way to go. He figured to make his way back to Cross River, rest up a day or two, resupply, and then head out again. He was pretty sure that he would head right back up here to Jacksontown, as he came to see it. This village strung out along both sides of the Clear Boggy would indeed be the place to come looking around again. But next time, Calhoun would not be so open about it.

With such thoughts in mind, he moved a little faster. Sometime in the afternoon of the day after next, he hit the stage road and followed it southwestward. He took the ferry, scowling every time he saw the owner, Ben Colbert. Even though Colbert was a Chickasaw, not a Choctaw, Calhoun did not care. As far as he was concerned right now, an Indian was an Indian, and the Chickasaws were closely akin to the Choctaws, as far as Calhoun could tell.

As he left the ferry and began the short ride to Cross River, he tried to put those thoughts from his mind. Instead, he began replacing them with thoughts of Irene McGowan.

By the time he got into town, he was thinking of little else, but he figured he had better stop by and talk with Ferguson before going to see Irene. He did not look forward to it, but on the other hand, he was not about to take any abuse from Ferguson or anyone else right now. He stopped at the stage office, dismounted, and went inside.

C H A P T E R

∗ 11 ∗

Irene was waiting for Calhoun in the sitting room,
though she was trying to pretend she had not been.
She smiled warmly and even managed a small look
of surprise when Calhoun walked in. "You must be
tired and hungry," she said, rising and walking toward
him. "Would you like something to eat? I have some
ham I can warm up for you."

Calhoun nodded. "Coffee, too?" he asked hopefully.

"Of course."

Calhoun nodded again. "I'm gonna go wash up a little," he said tiredly.

"All right. I'll have things ready for you . . . in the
kitchen." Irene suddenly looked embarrassed.

"Thanks." Calhoun clumped upstairs. He poured
some water into the basin and washed his hands and
face. Looking into the mirror hanging on the wall above
the basin, he grimaced. He was never one for much
neatness, but his scruffy beard annoyed him now for
some reason. He figured that reason was working now
down in the kitchen, but he wasn't about to admit it,
even to himself. He soaped up the growth and swiftly
scratched it off with a straight razor.

Done, he looked at himself in the mirror. He thought

it little improvement overall, but there was nothing he could do about that, not after all these years. He shrugged, dried himself off, and headed downstairs.

Calhoun had forgotten how good a cook Irene McGowan was, and he wolfed down the excellent meal and three cups of coffee. After more than a week of his own cooking—and the wretched slop that Elva Templeton had foisted on him—it was a pure joy to eat something that tasted like food. After finishing, he pushed back his chair a little. "My, but that was good, ma'am," he said.

Irene flushed with pride. "More coffee, Wade?"

Calhoun nodded.

"Pie? It's pecan."

Calhoun nodded again.

After Irene had put a large slice of pie in front of Calhoun and refilled his coffee cup, she asked, "Would you like a little strengthener for that coffee, Wade?"

Calhoun looked at her in a little surprise. "I'd be obliged," he offered.

Irene smiled, a little discomfited. "My husband would like that of a time, Wade," she said only a little sadly. "I figure most men do. I usually keep a small bottle hidden away for such times." She smiled again, weakly this time. "I ain't had a chance to use it . . . since . . . since Johnny . . ."

"There's no need to say more, Irene. If it bothers you, I can do without."

"No, no, that's all right. I just hope it's still good." She brushed away the few tears that had come unbidden, and she was smiling when she turned back to the table with the pint bottle of whiskey. She poured a good amount in Calhoun's coffee.

Calhoun tasted it and pronounced it just right. Then he dug into the pie. Finally, though, he was finished, feeling almost bloated. He rolled a cigarette, which he puffed while he drank the last of his spiked coffee.

"Would you like to go into the sitting room a while, Wade?" Irene asked a little nervously.

Calhoun shrugged and nodded. He rose and escorted Irene into the sitting room and took a seat opposite her. He stretched his legs out, comfortable but wary. He was facing the door, his back to the wall, so he could see anyone coming and going.

"That young feller been botherin' you any?"

"Alvin Webb?"

Calhoun nodded.

"He's not really been botherin' me any. He still likes to sit down here with me of an evenin' though."

"That all right by you?"

Irene nodded. "I'd . . . well, I'd rather have you sittin' here with me, like this, but if you're not around . . ."

Calhoun nodded. "I won't be around much again. Just a couple of days."

"Will you sit with me sometimes while you're in town?"

"I'd be pleased, ma'am." Actually, he'd much rather be over in a saloon or a brothel. But Irene McGowan was too nice a woman to treat so callously, so he sat.

Irene kept trying to draw some talk out of Calhoun, but had little success. Finally he said to her, "Sorry, Irene, but I ain't much given to conversin' at the best of times."

She nodded, a little sad about that.

"I don't mind if you talk at me, though, Irene," Calhoun said, figuring that would make her feel better.

She smiled wanly. "You sure you don't mind me prattlin' on, Mister Calhoun?" She was unsure of herself.

"No, ma'am. I don't figure any man'd get tired of hearin' your voice."

Irene blushed. "Why, thank you, Wade." She paused and then started talking, softly, sometimes earnestly, sometimes with an added giggle or two.

Calhoun paid little attention to it, since most of what Irene had to say was of little interest to him. He did note that she mentioned somewhere in her meandering monologue that two men—a Chris Graham and Doug Talbot—had moved into the boardinghouse a few days ago. He also noted that she did not like them much. Or maybe it was that she feared them too much. He vowed silently to find out who the men were, what they were doing in Cross River, and warn them to leave Irene alone. He grimaced inwardly as he thought how his life had come down to issuing warnings to men to keep away from a woman who meant little more than an evening's dull companionship. Perhaps if she were a little more free with her favors, he might not see the task as such a demeaning one, but he could not expect that of a sheltered woman like Irene McGowan.

Occasionally, he nodded or shrugged, grunted an affirmative or negative, even ventured an "Is that so?" every once in a while. Because of that, she seemed to think that he was paying her all his attention. He did not disillusion her.

Finally Irene began winding down, and eventually she stopped talking. She smiled ruefully. "I know I've ruined your evening, Wade," she said quietly, a little abashed, "but I'm mighty obliged to you for humorin' me. It's not often I can just set with a man and talk. Seems like near every man I meet thinks that because I've been married and have known a man's intimacies, that I'm open to the same with anyone who comes along. But I ain't like that, Wade."

"I know," he said softly. *All too well,* he thought.

"I thought at first that you'd be such a man to try those things," Irene said boldly.

Calhoun shrugged. "I ain't ever been the type to force myself on a woman."

"I'm pleased. And, again, Wade, thanks for lettin' me blather on." She rose. "I imagine you'd like to visit a saloon for a while and hear the coarse talk of other men," she said with a smile.

Calhoun nodded.

"Don't you ever smile, Mister Calhoun?" Irene suddenly asked. "Or laugh?"

"No, ma'am," he answered honestly.

"Why not?"

"It's of no interest to you, Irene," Calhoun said gruffly.

"Oh, but it is."

Calhoun shook his head. "I got my reasons, ma'am."

Irene nodded sadly. "I understand. Well, I must get to bed. My mornin' comes early, when I have to be makin' breakfast for all my boarders. Good night, Wade, and thank you."

"My pleasure, ma'am."

Calhoun spent the next day wandering around town. He visited one of the brothels for a spell, and then spent some time talking with Henry Ferguson over at the stage office. It was a hot, humid day, one which made Calhoun feel mighty lazy.

In the afternoon, he went to the Staghorn. The saloon was more along the lines of places he liked than was the Red River or several of the other saloons in Cross River. The Staghorn was a sinkhole, foul smelling and filled with rough characters. Calhoun felt right at home in such a place. He whiled away the afternoon drinking rye and doing little else.

He finally managed to rouse himself in the late afternoon. He had about an hour to kill before Irene would serve supper, so he thought he might go back to his room and nap a little. He had had enough whiskey to make him feel a little light-headed, though he was not drunk. A nap would make him feel better, he figured.

Calhoun entered the boardinghouse and stopped in the hallway when he heard a crash from somewhere upstairs. Then he heard Irene scream, a sound that was swiftly muffled. He sprinted down the hall and took the stairs to the second floor three at a time. Without slowing, he smashed through Irene's door, stumbling a little as the wood burst and fell inward.

With one swift glance, he took in the entire tableau. A battered, unconscious Alvin Webb lay on the floor near one wall. Irene was on the bed, struggling as two men tried to remove her clothes. Both looked up in surprise when Calhoun rammed his way into the room.

"Son of a bitch," one said. He began turning, leaving his companion to continue holding Irene down. As he spun, his hand went for his holstered revolver.

Calhoun stepped up and pounded the man in the stomach with all his strength. The man doubled over, his face turning red. Calhoun whirled and grabbed the other attacker by the back of the collar and the seat of the pants. He spun the man away from Irene, then shoved him forward as hard as he could.

The man—Chris Graham—lurched forward, unable to stop himself. The wall brought him to a halt, only inches from the window that overlooked the back yard. Calhoun glanced at the other man—Doug Talbot. Seeing that Talbot was not going to do anything for at least a few more moments, Calhoun moved forward and hammered Graham several punches in the kidney area. Then he grabbed the back of Graham's head, pulled it back, and then smashed it forward into the wall twice.

Graham moaned and slid down the wall.

Calhoun turned. Talbot was still doubled over, but was showing signs of life. Calhoun hustled over there, winking at Irene, on the way. He grabbed Talbot by the scruff of the collar and the seat of the pants. He spun Talbot and then launched him.

Two feet from there, Talbot's head smashed through the room's other window. Calhoun kicked Talbot in the rump and shoved. The impetus pushed Talbot out the window. He landed in a thudding pile of breaking bones on the dusty alley below.

Calhoun stuck his head out the window and looked. If Talbot wasn't dead, he was sure in some bad shape, Calhoun figured. He would cause no more trouble.

"Wade!" Irene screamed.

Calhoun whirled, his right hand automatically latching onto one of his Dragoons. By the time he was facing Graham, the pistol was in his hand.

Graham had managed to get up and draw his own

pistol. His pains made him unsteady, but he was determined to shoot the son of a bitch who had interfered with his and his friend's entertainments.

"One chance," Calhoun growled.

"Kiss my ass," Graham barked angrily, blood from his two loosened teeth and his dripping nose spraying out with the words.

Calhoun shot him twice—once in the center of the chest, once in the forehead.

Graham toppled without a sound.

"You all right?" Calhoun asked, turning to Irene.

She nodded tentatively, then more firmly. She got off the bed and came to him. She wrapped her arms around his middle and lay a cheek against his chest.

Against his better judgment, Calhoun brought his arms around Irene's small shoulders and held her tight. She seemed to melt against him. Finally, though, he pushed her gently away. "Things've got to be done, Irene," he said firmly.

She parted reluctantly from him and nodded.

"You got a doc in town?" Calhoun asked.

Irene nodded. "Are you hurt?" she asked, still rattled by all that had gone on here.

"Nope. Mister Webb is, though, and he can use the doc's services. How'd he get here?"

"He must've seen or heard somethin'. The door wasn't locked, and he suddenly barged in. While Mister Talbot held on to me—in a most obscene and unwelcome manner—Mister Graham beat poor Alvin to pulp there. Then he came back and he and . . ."

"Hush." He walked to the window and looked out. Several people were standing or kneeling around Talbot's body. Some were looking at the corpse; the others were looking up. "One of you go get the doc. And somebody get the undertaker," Calhoun ordered.

Calhoun pulled his head back inside, walked to Webb, and knelt next to him.

Webb moaned a little, which Calhoun figured was good since it seemed to indicate that Webb was coming around.

A few minutes later, Doctor Royal Farnsworth hurried in. While the physician worked on Webb, Calhoun went to the window again and looked out. The undertaker was dealing with Talbot's body. "There's another up here, Mister Swain," Calhoun called out.

Josiah Swain looked up and nodded.

Calhoun looked at Irene. "You might not want to, but I figure it's best you went downstairs and got supper ready. There's other boarders who've got to eat. And it'll help you keep your mind off what's gone on in here."

Irene nodded dumbly. The thought of food right now disgusted her, but Calhoun was right.

"And get someone to come fix this door right off."

Irene nodded again and shuffled out of the room. Calhoun followed her and went to his room.

CHAPTER

* 12 *

Two nights later a noise woke Calhoun in the middle of the night. His hand went for one of his Dragoons, hanging in their holsters from the short bedpost. He rolled out of bed to the floor, where he crouched, thumb on the hammer of the Colt.

The sound came again, and Calhoun knew someone was trying to open his door, which he had locked as he always did. Then there was nothing for some little time.

Calhoun had just relaxed and stood, ready to put the pistol away when the noise came again. Swiftly he glided on bare feet to the wall next to the door. He waited, uncocked revolver held upward next to his head.

The door opened and Irene McGowan walked in. She, too, was barefoot, and she wore only a thin, cotton nightdress. She stopped and let her eyes adjust to the darkness of the room after the lantern-lit hallway. She froze when she realized Calhoun was not in his bed.

"Howdy," Calhoun said quietly from behind her.

Irene jumped a little, then turned slowly. She smiled when she saw him. "Plannin' to shoot me, Mister Cal-

103

houn?" she asked in a husky voice that Calhoun had never heard her use before.

"Not with this," Calhoun said bluntly, lowering the pistol. "What're you doing here, ma'am?"

"I . . . I . . ." Suddenly Irene felt cold inside, and thought herself a fool for having thought to come here.

"Do you know what this looks like?" Calhoun demanded, though not harshly.

Irene nodded, not sure she would be able to speak again just yet.

"You sure that's what you want?"

Irene nodded again, but it was accompanied by a smile this time. She moved very close to him and looked up into his hard face. "Even a good woman, a chaste woman, needs a man's intimate touch of a time," she said, her voice a combination of husky desire and fearful innocence.

"I expect they do," Calhoun said. He wrapped his left arm around her and pulled her tight against him. Then he kissed her hard. When they broke apart, he swept her off her feet and carried her to the bed, where he playfully dropped her. He slid his pistol away, lit a lantern, which he put on low, and closed and locked the door.

"You going to take all night?" Irene asked, half brazenly, half fearfully. She was still afraid he might reject her. Or use her and then cast her aside.

"No, ma'am," Calhoun said as he joined her on the bed.

"The lantern?" she asked tentatively.

"We got to see what we're doin'."

Irene sighed and relaxed as Calhoun's hands began expertly roaming her body.

✳   ✳   ✳

Calhoun was just eating his breakfast in the morning when Henry Ferguson charged into the boardinghouse dining room. He was highly agitated. "There you are, dammit," he said in exasperation when he spotted Calhoun.

Calhoun looked at him in surprise.

"Come on, Wade, you've got to ride."

"Where and why?"

"More horses stolen," Ferguson said, puffing some. "Down at Templeton's station. Just a few days ago. You've got to get down there and start trackin' those bastards. If . . ."

"Mister Ferguson," Irene said icily, rising from her chair to glare at him. "You are, I know, an important man in Cross River. But this is my home, and I will not have such language used here."

"Yes'm," Ferguson muttered. He looked back at Calhoun. "Now, Wade . . ."

"Sit," Calhoun commanded. "Have some coffee or somethin'."

"But . . ."

"Look, Henry, those horse thieves've got four days' head start, maybe more. Another hour ain't gonna make a bit of difference." He paused for a mouthful of eggs. "Now sit and have some coffee. Miz McGowan might even let you eat some. While you're at it, tell me what you know."

Ferguson looked flustered and almost helpless for a few moments. Then he regained control of himself and sat. Irene placed a cup of coffee and a plate of eggs and bacon in front of him. It smelled good, he realized, remembering that he had not had anything to eat yet today. He dug in.

He spoke around mouthfuls of food. "We just got word that the thieves hit Templeton's place again. Ran off every head of stock he had. Horses, mules, even the damned cow." He looked a little defiantly at Irene, who smiled sweetly back at him.

"Anyway," Ferguson continued gruffly, "Charlie Endicott and Fred Waverly had to make the run to here with the horses they had. Drove two nights to get here."

"Any idea who did it?"

"The Comanches. Who else? Nobody else'd have audacity to pull somethin' like that."

Calhoun nodded. "I'll pull out soon's I get ready."

"Good. Anything I can do to help?"

"Have someone go over to Fleming's and get me some supplies. The usual. Bacon, beans, jerky. Enough for a couple of days."

Ferguson nodded. He gulped down the last of his meal and coffee, then jumped up, and hustled out.

Calhoun and Irene were alone in the dining room. Those few lingerers who had been around when Ferguson had huffed in were not of a mood to sit and listen to him spout off, and they had rapidly drifted off.

"Do you have to leave already?" Irene asked, trying not to sound disappointed.

Calhoun nodded.

"You don't have any time at all?"

"Some. Why?" He followed her eyes as they went upward. "In the daylight?" he asked.

"You ashamed?"

Calhoun shook his head. "No, ma'am. Concerned about your reputation."

"I'll survive it," Irene said flatly. The attack on her by Graham and Talbot the other day had changed her. She was no longer willing to accept what others said she was to be or how she was supposed to act. Not entirely anyway.

Calhoun nodded. They rose and walked upstairs together.

Forty minutes later, Calhoun was riding out of Cross River, heading southwest. He wasted no time, traveling long hours, stopping as infrequently as possible. He reached Templeton's station late in the afternoon the day after leaving Cross River.

He did not sit on the ridge and survey the place this time. He just rode straight on down. With no animals in the corral, the place looked deserted, but then he spotted Templeton working outside. Templeton saw him and waited for him to arrive.

"Welcome back, Mister Calhoun," Templeton said.

Calhoun nodded.

"You hungry?" Elva Templeton asked, coming out side.

Calhoun's stomach lurched, but he nodded. He needed food and, though he was not sure that what Elva supplied would qualify, it would fill his stomach. He figured that if he could keep it down, it would do him some good.

"I hope you catch the bastards this time," Templeton said as the three walked inside.

Calhoun nodded again. He sat and forced down the slop Elva slapped on a tin plate for him and choked back a cup of coffee. "Which way'd they go this time?" he asked after eating. He already could hear his stomach starting to protest the strains he had just placed on it. "North again?"

"Dewey followed the tracks a little, didn't you, boy?" Templeton smiled proudly at his son. "They went west."

"Comanches?" Calhoun asked.

"Yep," Dewey said.

Calhoun stared evenly at him. There was something about Dewey Templeton that Calhoun just did not like. And he was suspicious. It seemed to Calhoun that Dewey was fighting off a smirk. Then Calhoun shrugged mentally. He was probably just making these things up out of his frustration.

"How many?" Calhoun asked.

"Six. Eight, maybe," Dewey said.

"And they didn't attack the station itself?"

"Nope," Templeton said. "It was the damnedest thing, too, to my thinkin'. They know there's only the three of us here. They got to know that."

"C'mon, Pa," Dewey said with a snort, "ain't no one of us can know what goes on in the heads of those savages."

"That's a fact," Templeton agreed. "It sure is." He looked at Calhoun. "When're you fixin' to leave?"

"First thing in the mornin'. I pushed hard to get here, and my horse needs rest."

"Well, you can spend the night here, no problem," Templeton said. "Right, Dear?"

"Absolutely," Elva said. "We wouldn't have it any other way. I'll fix you up a bed special."

Calhoun almost cringed at the thought. He considered sleeping outside in his bedroll. That would keep most of the lice and bedbugs off him. The thought was mighty tempting, but with Comanches on the prowl, there was little safety enough inside. Outside there would be none at all. He nodded.

"Anything you need for tomorrow?" Templeton asked.

"Just some cigarette fixin's, if you got extra."

"We got plenty." Templeton rose and went to the back of the big room. Boxes and bales were piled up there. He poked through one and then returned to the table. He tossed a pouch of tobacco, a package of wheatstraw papers, and two boxes of matches on the table. "That do you?" he asked.

Calhoun nodded and rose. "Well, I'd best see to my horse and then hit the hay."

"Dewey'll take care of your horse, if you want, Mister Calhoun," Templeton said.

Calhoun shook his head. "I can do it."

He rode out the next morning, another foul mass of gruel churning in his stomach. He itched all over, too, and swore silently at it. He headed west, and two miles away from Templeton's, he started looking at the ground. He wanted to track the Comanches, but he also had another reason.

Less than an hour later, he saw what he was looking for. He rode a few feet beyond it and dismounted. He loosened the saddle and hobbled the bay with the reins. Then he pulled off all his clothes, walked back to the cluster of large anthills he had seen and laid the clothes over them.

He felt like a complete idiot, standing there buck naked except for his gun belt, picking lice and bedbugs off his skin while waiting for the ants to devour the vermin infesting his clothes.

Calhoun felt a lot better, though, after he had dressed. The ants had done a good job, and he had plucked off quite a few. He believed he was almost entirely free of the annoying little vermin.

Relieved of that nagging annoyance, he could concentrate more on tracking. He stopped several times in the next few miles, checking the ground closely. He was out in the short grass prairie now, where nothing but the wind could've disturbed hoof tracks. There had been no rain, and the ground was dusty and soft enough to leave a decent trail. Trouble was, he couldn't find a trail.

He finally stopped and stood there, thinking it over. He was an excellent tracker, and it bothered him considerably that he found no sign of the stolen horses being taken this way. With his skills, if he couldn't find the trail left by fifteen or twenty stolen horses, plus another half-dozen or so Indian ponies ridden by the raiders, then he was either losing his skills, or the raiders had not come this way. He finally decided it was the latter. He mounted up and rode back the way he had come.

He got almost all the way back to Templeton's station and still had not found the trail. He stopped again, smoking a cigarette as he pondered his next move. It was possible, though highly unlikely that the Comanches had gone east. Unless they were planning more raids that way. A more likely direction, Calhoun figured, would be south. Places to raid were a lot more common that way than they were to the east or west.

There was always the north, of course, he knew. Up that way were Indians the Comanches probably could—and would—trade with. Indians like the Choctaws. He was tempted to head straight north, but he battled down the impulse. He decided that he would head south a little; not more than a few miles. If he found nothing there, he would go east and circle around back toward Templeton's. Since they were unlikely directions, they could be covered quickly. If he picked up the trail, so much the better. If he didn't, the north always beckoned.

Mind made up, he wasted no more time. He tightened his saddle and then was off. Three miles south, he had found no trail, so he swung to the east and stopped for the night.

In the morning, he rode northeast, weaving back and forth, eyes searching the ground. When he was almost back at Templeton's once again, he decided that north would have to be the way he went. He picked up speed then, figuring he really didn't need to find the trail. Not until he crossed the Red River anyway.

Once he got across the river, he rode east, following the bank of the Red. There was no trail to be found after a day's ride that way, so he turned westward, again following the riverbank, past where he had started and then farther west. His frustration began to grow. He had ridden out of Cross River more than a week ago, and he was no closer to finding the horse thieves than he had been when he left.

Then he spotted what he thought might be what he sought. It turned north and slightly east. He nodded, figuring the trail would lead him right back to Jacksontown on the Clear Boggy River. He moved with more speed and assurance.

He rode into the Choctaw village two days later, and was surprised to find an army patrol camping nearby. That did not bother him too much, though he was concerned that they might've caught the horse thieves, and he would get no reward. It bothered him even less when he found out who was commanding it. He had scouted for Captain Marcus Clifton back before the raid on his Kansas Territory farm.

He stopped near Clifton's tent, which was set off from those of his troops by some yards and a small screen of brush.

CHAPTER

* 13 *

"**W**hat're you doing here, Calhoun?" Clifton asked with a small grin.

Calhoun shook his head. "Trackin' horse thieves."

"You never did have any luck with horses," Clifton said. "Come on and sit. Have some coffee."

Calhoun sat on a folding, canvas camp chair across the small fire from Clifton. "These ain't mine." When Clifton looked at him in question, Calhoun added, "Henry Ferguson hired me."

"I'd heard Butterfield was losing a lot of stock," Clifton said with a nod. "Who do you think's behind it?"

"Comanches," Calhoun said flatly.

"You're in the wrong neck of the woods for Comanches, boy," Clifton said, eyebrows raised in surprise.

Calhoun nodded. "I think they're sellin' 'em to the Choctaws and others up this way."

"That could be. You got any proof?"

"None other than I found a couple of the Butterfield horses in a corral over in yon town a week or so ago." He pointed toward Jacksontown.

"That doesn't mean the Comanches took them. Could've been the Choctaws themselves. Or even

113

white men who sold them here."

"The chief here said it was a white man. I don't believe him."

"He say who it was?" Clifton knew Calhoun's long-standing hatred of all Indians, and he was not about to argue with him over it. Not just yet anyway.

"Somebody named Micah Alexander."

"He's a bad one, Wade."

"You know him?" Calhoun asked, surprised. He had been so sure that the Choctaw chief had lied to him that he had not even considered the possibility of Alexander being real, let alone the head of the horse thieves.

"Know of him. He's wanted from Independence to San Antonio for all sorts of things. Mostly horse theft, though. And robbing stages."

"He operate around here?" Calhoun was still surprised but was beginning to accept the possibility that Alexander might be the culprit. Not that he believed it yet.

"Sure. Every time we're on patrol we've got our eyes peeled for him and his pack of wolves. Never have been able to run him down, though."

"You spot him, try to get word to me through Ferguson. I want to talk to him."

"You haven't changed your thinking, though, have you?" Clifton asked with a grin.

"About the Indians? Hell, no."

"Didn't think so. I'll keep my eyes open around here and in Chickasaw territory, too, and see if I can learn anything. Hell, I wouldn't put it past these Indians—or any goddamn redskins—to either be stealing the horses themselves or buying them from the thieves with the full knowledge that they're stolen."

Calhoun nodded. "You stayin' here long?" he asked.

"Nah. Just the night. Maybe tomorrow, too. We've got no real reason to be here. We're just on routine patrol and're checking things over." He paused. "You're welcome to sup with me tonight and spend the night here, if you're of a mind."

"I'll do that."

Calhoun went off and tended to his horse. Then he wandered through the village, knowing that once again he was being watched. He stopped by George Franklin's place. The corral had been fixed, but there were no new horses in it. Franklin was standing by the log barn watching him. He touched his hat brim in Franklin's direction, but when it was returned, he realized that Franklin could not have gotten the sarcasm the gesture was meant to have.

Soon after, Calhoun ate supper with Clifton and then dawdled over cigars and coffee with the officer. Finally, though, he rose. "Well, Cap'n, I think I'll go nose around the village some more, then hit the hay."

Clifton nodded. "Breakfast tomorrow here?"

Calhoun nodded and walked off. Dark was rapidly gathering, and lights were flickering on in the Choctaws' cabins. He stopped in the shadow of a cottonwood when he saw a young woman framed in the light of a cabin doorway as she came out. Calhoun knew she was an Indian, but from this short distance, she appeared to be a rather attractive young woman. She moved through the trees toward the Clear Boggy not far away. For some reason he could not fathom, Calhoun followed her at a respectful distance.

He suddenly heard her—or some other woman— screech. He trotted forward, not wanting to go too fast, since it was very dark in the cover of the trees. He almost stumbled on two men who had the woman on the ground near the bank of the creek.

"Jesus," Calhoun cursed silently. He was getting in the habit of rescuing women, and was not sure he liked it. He stalked forward and kicked the nearest man in the rump.

The man jumped and spun his head. "Goddamn!" he snapped. "You again, you son of a bitch."

Calhoun nodded at former First Sergeant—now Staff Sergeant—Paul Thatcher. "I see your jaw's healed up," he said noncommittally. "Too bad." He kicked Thatcher in the underside of the jaw, knocking him back into the other man.

That man had turned when Thatcher had first spoken. Calhoun saw that the onetime sergeant was now Corporal Curtis Williamson. He went sprawling as Thatcher bounced into him.

Both soldiers tried to get up, as the young woman scrambled out from beneath them.

"You're gonna die now, you nose-buttin'-in son of a bitch," Williamson said as he got to his feet. Thatcher was right beside him, looking to be in considerable pain. They started moving forward, toward Calhoun, separating a little as they walked.

Calhoun drew one of the Dragoons. Everyone froze.

"Shit," Williamson said, "you ain't gonna shoot a couple of Uncle Sam's boys." He began moving forward again, though Thatcher stayed where he was.

Calhoun calmly shot him twice in the chest. Williamson fell in a heap, the look of surprise and shock in his eyes fading fast in the new night's starlight.

Thatcher's eyes widened in surprise, too. Then he whirled and raced toward the young woman. He tackled her. Getting an arm around her throat, he struggled to his feet, pulling her with him. At the same time, he started scrabbling with his flap holster, going for his gun.

The woman bit him on the forearm where his shirt-sleeve was rolled up some. She also dug her fingernails into the arm.

Thatcher roared in pain and jerked his arm away from her throat. The woman flopped to the ground, and Calhoun immediately fired twice again. One ball hit Thatcher in the throat, the other in the cheek. He toppled onto his back.

Calhoun could hear people hurrying toward them as he walked to the woman. He dropped the Dragoon into its holster and pulled the other, just in case. Then he helped the woman up. Even in the darkness he could see that she was attractive. It annoyed him when he felt a flash of excitement inside at her nearness. He couldn't have any desire for an Indian woman, no matter how good-looking or pleasant she might be. He just would not—could not—allow that.

Several armed Choctaws burst into the little clearing by the creek, and suddenly Calhoun found a number of cocked pistols and rifles pointed at him.

"No!" the woman said, stepping in front of him. She spoke in her own language, voice fast and harsh. She was in the middle of her address when the chief, Sam Jackson, came along. The woman stopped speaking, then began again at a nod from Jackson.

By the time she finished, Captain Marcus Clifton and a few soldiers had arrived. "What the hell's going on here?" he asked. Then he spotted the bodies. He went to them one at a time, kneeling to make sure they were dead. Then he stood and looked at Calhoun. "Wade?"

"I caught 'em tryin' to debase this woman," Calhoun said flatly. "When I stopped 'em, they came at me."

"You killed two soldiers—two *United States* soldiers—over the 'honor' of a goddamn squaw?" Clifton snapped.

Calhoun nodded.

"I thought you hated all Indians?" Clifton was incredulous.

"I do."

"Then why this?" He waved a hand vaguely.

"I don't cotton to any woman bein' treated in such a way."

"But . . ."

Calhoun threw caution to the winds. "This ain't the first time I caught these two at such a thing," he said flatly. "It appears that's the only way they could get a woman, since the last time they tried it, they were attackin' a strumpet."

"That's no reason to . . ." Suddenly he clamped his mouth shut as his eyes widened in the shock of recognition. "You were the one killed Lieutenant Peters and Sergeant Coble in that whorehouse," he said.

Calhoun nodded. "Beat the snot out of these two, too."

"Damn, Wade," Clifton said in annoyance, recovering from his shock a little, "this puts me in an awkward spot. Lord knows, these two weren't no great loss— hell, if you noticed, they were busted in rank. That was because of the fracas back in Fort Smith. Peters and Coble weren't much either, but goddamn, Wade, how'm I going to explain to the commander that you killed three sergeants. . . ."

"Two sergeants and a corporal," Calhoun corrected.

"All right, two sergeants and a corporal. *Plus* a lieutenant. And all because you were trying to protect a whore and a goddamn Indian?"

Calhoun shrugged. "That's your problem."

Clifton sighed and shook his head. He had his duty to do, and he was going to do it. "I'm afraid I'm going to have to arrest you, Wade. Much as I might hate to. Men," he ordered, "place Mister Calhoun under arrest."

The soldiers edged forward warily, seeing as how Calhoun still had his Colt pistol in hand. They brought their rifles to bear on him. They had only taken a few steps, though, when Jackson barked some kind of order, and the Choctaws surged forward, getting between Calhoun and the soldiers. The troops stopped, looking worriedly from the Indians to their commander.

"You willin' to start a war, Captain?" Jackson asked.

Clifton looked apoplectic, but managed to calm himself. He smiled ruefully. "No, Chief Jackson. I sure ain't."

"We'll watch over Mister Calhoun until you and your men leave here in the mornin'."

Clifton nodded. He glanced toward Calhoun. "We'll meet up again, Wade. Soon."

"You trouble Mister Calhoun while he's in Choctaw country, Captain," Jackson said flatly, "and I'll consider it an act of war."

Clifton glared at him for some moments, then nodded. "You would, too, you wily old son of a bitch." He grinned lopsidedly. He turned to his men. "Any of you want to start a war over the likes of those two?" He pointed toward the bodies. When he got no affirmative response, he nodded and looked at Jackson. "You mind if we bury our men somewhere hereabouts?"

Jackson shook his head. "Just don't make it too close to Boggy Hollow."

Clifton nodded. "Well, I'm deeply grieved to have lost two fine soldiers in the assault on that outlaw encampment a few miles from the Choctaw town of Boggy Hollow. It was a horrific fight," he added, head bobbing up and down as the story took shape. "But we finally prevailed at the end, saving Boggy Hollow from certain devastation."

Jackson permitted himself a small smile.

Clifton looked at Calhoun. "Good luck, Wade," he said.

Calhoun nodded, then asked, "Your word you and the others won't come after me?"

"My word," Clifton said without hesitation. "And I'll personally flog the son of a bitch under my command who spills the beans."

Calhoun nodded.

A moment later, Clifton directed his soldiers to sling their rifles and carry the two bodies back to their camp.

When the soldiers were gone, the Choctaws relaxed a little. Jackson looked at Calhoun. "Thank you for saving my granddaughter, Mister Calhoun," he said with dignity. "I wouldn't have expected such a thing from a man like you."

"Didn't much expect it myself," Calhoun said truthfully.

"I understand," Jackson said. He paused. "You'll be my guest tonight, Mister Calhoun," he said, making it sound like an order.

Calhoun nodded, knowing he had little choice.

Jackson suddenly let out a little laugh. "This's really somethin', ain't it, Mister Calhoun?" he said. "The Indian hater being protected from his own people by the Indians."

Calhoun did not appreciate the irony and saw no humor in the situation. "I need to get my horse and supplies," he said tightly.

"We'll see to it." Jackson issued some commands in his native language, and Franklin and another Choctaw left. "Come, Mister Calhoun," Jackson said, turning and walking off.

Calhoun shrugged, holstered his revolver and followed.

The house was larger than any of the others Calhoun had seen here. A number of rooms had been added over the years, giving the building a rather odd look. Each room addition had its own character, and while they all fit together well, they didn't completely match, making the exterior of the house look like a patchwork quilt. Nearby was a planed log barn with a fenced-in corral, and a small, rough-looking log building that Calhoun figured housed some slaves.

Calhoun waited outside until his horse and supplies were brought. The Choctaws had set his saddle across the horse's back but had not tightened it in any way. Calhoun took the saddle and slung it over the top rail of the corral fence.

Then he looked the animal over well. With his luck with horses, he wouldn't be surprised if either the soldiers or the Choctaws hadn't done something to it in between the army camp and the Choctaw village. Everything seemed all right, though, and he turned the horse out into the corral. Then he nodded to Jackson who was waiting by his doorway.

The old chief went inside, followed by the Choctaw Calhoun didn't know, then Calhoun himself, and finally Franklin, who was carrying Calhoun's saddlebags and canvas sack of supplies.

CHAPTER

* 14 *

Calhoun found Jackson's house to be a lot more clean, comfortable, and pleasant smelling than Templeton's station house was. It was more crowded, though, what with Jackson, his old wife and her sister, Jackson's two daughters and their husbands, plus the young woman Calhoun had rescued and two other, younger grandchildren living inside the sprawling log house.

The place seemed warm and comfortable. It did have some smells that were odd to Calhoun, but not many. The room he was in was large and had a long table, much like the stage stations did. The kitchen area was roomy and had a huge cast-iron stove along one wall. The end of the room opposite the kitchen area was the sitting area, and there were a number of chairs as well as rugs scattered around.

Jackson had sent someone inside before to warn his family that they would have a guest—and why. So the entire family was standing in waiting when Calhoun stepped inside.

Calhoun did not like all the attention, and he could not memorize any of the names that were spouted off. Except one. The young woman he had rescued was named Winona Marshall.

Sitting at the table with a cup of coffee in front of him and Jackson across from him, Calhoun was able to get a good look at Winona. Like most of the other Choctaws Calhoun had seen, she was short and somewhat slender. Her skin was not nearly as dark as Jackson's and she had few Indian features that Calhoun could see. Her eyes were almost black, and they sparkled in the lantern light. Her pitch black hair was parted in the center and hung in a straight cascade to the middle of her back. She had thick eyebrows, long, soft lashes, prominent cheekbones, and a long, thin nose. Her lower lip was full and held a lot of promise, while her upper lip was just a thin strip of soft red.

All in all, Calhoun found her quite attractive, and could almost forget that she was an Indian at all. That displeased him, and he tried to force himself to think of Irene McGowan. He did not love Irene, but she was his latest bed partner and so freshest in his mind. Except for Lizbeth, of course, but thoughts of her would only put him in a murderous rage directed at any Indians who were nearby. That would never do.

Calhoun sat silently, sipping coffee and smoking as the Choctaws talked in their own language. Since Winona and Jackson were doing most of the talking, Calhoun figured they were recounting his deed. Of course, he thought ruefully, they could as easily be insulting him. He didn't think that likely, though.

Calhoun paid little attention to the talk, but kept sweeping his gaze across Winona. He found that every time she looked at him, she smiled invitingly. Once more he found himself attracted to her and had to bat down the feeling.

Finally the Choctaws had their fill of gabbing, and they started moving off to their beds. Each family had its own room, added to the main structure as needed.

"My bed's in that room," Jackson said, pointing. "Me and my wife'll stay out here."

"No," Calhoun said flatly. It was bad enough they were keeping him here to protect him from the soldiers, but he'd be damned before he threw the old couple out of their bed.

"But . . ."

"But nothin', Chief. I got my bedroll and I'm used to sleepin' on the ground. I'll be fine out here." He didn't want to sit here and argue about it either, so he stood, strode to his supplies, and got his bedroll. He went to the sitting room area, moved a couple of chairs and then unfurled his bedroll on the floor atop a rug.

Jackson shrugged and stood. Then he and his wife went into their room.

Once he was alone, Calhoun sat in a chair and pulled off his boots. He undid his gun belt and folded it so that one of the Colt Dragoons was available to him, and set it next to his bedroll, where it was in reach. The bowie knife went next to it. He pulled off his shirt and rolled it up to use it as a pillow. He decided to leave his pants on. He took out his backup gun and stuck it under the shirt. Finally he went around and blew out the three lanterns the others had left burning and then stretched out on the bedroll.

Thoughts of Lizbeth and Irene, and Winona made it hard for him to sleep, until he growled at himself to knock it off. At last he managed to blank the rampaging thoughts out, and he drifted off.

He was awake before anyone else had come into the

main room. He had dressed and was just finishing rolling up his bedroll when Winona came into the room. She was barefoot and still clad in her nightdress, the thickness of which revealed nothing of Winona's supple figure.

Winona strode boldly up to him, wrapped her small, delicate-looking hands around the back of his neck and pulled his head toward her. After which she planted an intriguing kiss on his mouth.

Calhoun responded in manly fashion, but then remembered who—or rather what—Winona was, and he pulled away.

Winona was a little surprised when he did, since she had been able to feel in his mouth—and elsewhere—that he had been reacting to her, but she shrugged it off for now. "That was my way of thankin' you for helpin' me last night," she said, still refusing to let go of the back of his neck.

"It was nothin'," Calhoun said gruffly, still fighting off the attraction of this woman. He brought his hands up and peeled hers away.

"Is there somethin' wrong with me?" Winona asked. She was not used to having men reject her. "Maybe you think I'm married or somethin'?"

"Nothin's wrong with you," Calhoun lied. "I got other things on my mind."

"Hogwash. I can tell what's on your mind." She grinned saucily.

"The others'll be along soon."

"So?"

"There's work to be done."

Winona gave up. She turned away. After putting the coffeepot on the stove, she went to her room and dressed. She looked prim and proper when she returned, and by then almost everyone else was up and about.

Before long, breakfast was served. Calhoun enjoyed it immensely. It had been a long time since he had had hominy. *Good* hominy, he corrected himself silently. With bacon and fresh biscuits, he remembered his childhood back in Tennessee. There had been little enough pleasure for him back then, and he had left home at seventeen to make his own way in the world. One of the few pleasures he could remember from that time was his mother's breakfasts.

After eating, the women drifted off to their chores and the children to play. The men sat at the table, smoking cigarettes or pipes, and sipping coffee.

"Well, I best be goin'," Calhoun said, rising.

"Sit a while longer," Jackson suggested.

"Can't. I got work to do."

"A few minutes won't make much difference."

"You makin' me your prisoner?" Calhoun demanded.

"No, Mister Calhoun," Jackson said quietly. "I just think you ought to give those soldiers some time to move on away from here before you leave."

Calhoun sat, nodding.

"I also suggest that when you do leave, that you take an escort with you."

Calhoun battled back the burst of fury. "You're gonna send 'em even if I don't want 'em, ain't you?" he asked calmly.

Jackson smiled and nodded.

Calhoun knew when he was beat. He rolled another cigarette.

★　　　★　　　★

Two hours later Calhoun was riding out of Boggy Hollow. Six well-armed, hard-eyed Choctaws accompanied him. Calhoun was disgusted at the thought of being accompanied by a half-dozen Indians, but he had little choice, unless he wanted to just kill all six. Well, he admitted to himself that he *did* want to do that, but he knew it was impossible.

Just before leaving, another Choctaw had come to Jackson's house and spoke with the old chief for a few minutes, both using their own language. When the man left, Jackson said to Calhoun, "The soldiers left just before dawn. They rode a mile south and buried the two men you killed last night. Then they continued south."

Calhoun nodded. "I'll head northeast some, till I cut the stage road. Then ride straight for Cross River."

Jackson nodded. "My men'll go with you as far as Colbert's Ferry."

Soon he and his unwanted escort left. They camped quite near the stage road that night. The next morning, Calhoun was up early. He had a built-in clock that allowed him to wake pretty much when he wanted, no matter how tired he was. So he woke an hour and a half before dawn. He took off his spurs and padded about the camp, trying to pack his supplies and saddle his horse without the others knowing about it.

But Zachary Marshall—Winona's father—suddenly appeared behind him and asked, "Leavin' us, Mister Calhoun?"

"Shit," Calhoun muttered. He turned. Marshall was not as tall as he was, but he was nearly as wiry and strong looking. His hair, eyes, and skin were dark. And he had a fairly decent mustache. "I was tryin' to get away from you and the others," he said bluntly.

"Why?" Marshall wiped sweat from his forehead on the sleeve of his cotton, white man's shirt. He also wore white man's denims, white man's plain black work boots, and a white man's hat. With cooler weather, he wore a brown, white man's coat, almost like a suit coat.

"'Cause I hate Indians," Calhoun said, thinking again of how little Marshall and all the other Choctaws looked like Indians.

"Why?"

"Because I do." Just because the Choctaws didn't *look* like Indians didn't mean they weren't Indians, Calhoun figured.

"All Indians?"

"Yep. Includin' busybody Choctaws."

"Then why'd you help my daughter?"

"I answered that last night."

"Not very well."

Calhoun sighed. "She's a woman before she's an Indian."

Marshall nodded. He thought it sad that a man with so much to give could be so closed off. But he knew there was nothing he could do to change Calhoun. "I'd be obliged if you didn't try this again, Mister Calhoun. I don't ask you to like us. I just ask that you let us do the task Chief Winter Bear has asked us to do."

"So that's the old bastard's name, eh? Winter Bear?"

Marshall nodded gravely. "He commands much respect among the Choctaws."

"I expect he does." Calhoun shrugged. "I won't try'n skip out on you no more. But leave me be."

Marshall nodded, but stood his ground. Only when Calhoun started walking back to the fire did the Choctaw move.

They saw no one else in the two days it took to get from Boggy Hollow to Colbert's Ferry. The Choctaws watched as Calhoun got on the ferry. When it began crossing the river, the Indians moved away, but not too far. Marshall and his men waited in the cover of some trees fifty yards from the ferry landing. Only when the ferry came back without Calhoun did they turn and head for home.

Ferguson seemed in a fairly good humor when Calhoun walked into the division superintendent's office.

"An army patrol was through here yesterday, heading south. The commander, a Captain Clifton, said he'd met up with you up in the Choctaw country."

Calhoun nodded and poured himself a drink of whiskey.

"Said you thought you were close to catching up to the Comanches that've been stealin' our horses." It was a question.

"No such luck."

"Dammit, Calhoun," Ferguson thundered, his good humor dying a quick and sudden death, "I hired you to stop the theft of Butterfield horses, not go wandering around in Choctaw country taking in the goddamn sights."

Calhoun swallowed the whiskey and then set the small glass on the desk. "One more insult, Ferguson," he said icily, "and I'll gut you."

Ferguson believed him, and began to sweat. "Have you learned anything?" he ventured nervously.

Calhoun shook his head. "Not a hell of a lot. I've followed the trail to Choctaw land, but I always lose the trail up there. I think the Choctaws're helpin' the damn

Comanches. Either that or the Comanches're splittin' into small parties once they cross the Red."

"You have any ideas?"

Calhoun shrugged. "I'll take a day or so here, then head back up to Choctaw land. Maybe I can find somethin'."

"I hope so."

Calhoun nodded and stood. "You know, Ferguson," he said slowly, "that if the Comanches're doin' this like we think they are, it might be impossible to catch them."

"I was afraid you were going to say that."

"About the only thing you could do then would be to hire a half-dozen guards for each station. Hit the Comanches hard whenever and wherever they raid."

"I don't want to even think about that," Ferguson said honestly. "Let's hope you can find them first."

Calhoun went out, took his horse to the livery and then headed for the boardinghouse. He was more than a little annoyed when he found Alvin Webb in the sitting room with Irene. The young man's face was still a mess of bruises, which went a long way in keeping Calhoun from pounding on him some more.

Irene jumped up and rushed to Calhoun, embracing him heartily. Calhoun got a moment of pleasure at seeing the hurt look on Webb's face when Irene did that.

Though supper had been over for a while, Irene went to make something just for Calhoun. Calhoun sat.

"How're you doin', boy?" he asked Webb.

"Middlin'," Webb answered honestly.

"Took a good thumpin', did you?"

"Yes, sir." Webb hung his head. "Miss Irene told me what you done. I'm obliged."

Calhoun nodded.

CHAPTER

* 15 *

Irene helped considerably in removing Calhoun's annoyance about Webb and Ferguson when she came to him that night. And the next two. She was loving and caring with him, which worried him a little. Only the lust that was obvious in her clear, green eyes kept him from thinking about the potential entanglements too much.

Finally, though, Calhoun knew he had to get on the trail again. So after one more libidinous night, he rode out of Cross River. Deciding that he had had no luck riding south, he crossed the Red River on Colbert's Ferry and headed northeast along the stage road. He hoped that by changing his route this time, he might be able to scare something—or someone—up. It was a risk, he figured, since the Comanches would be out west. He thought, though, that he might be able to catch some of the Indians selling horses to the Choctaws or the Chickasaws.

As he rode slowly up the road that morning, he also vowed that if he did not find anything solid on the Comanches this time, that he would give up the job. He was making no money anyway, and he could not see continuing to take Ferguson's supplies and such for nothing. He was not that kind of man.

He traveled northeast for three days, not pushing himself or the horse, since he saw no reason to do so. Finally he cut westward. On this course, he would pass north of Boggy Hollow, which suited him. He had no desire to go see Jackson's Choctaws. Despite their help, they were still Indians. He realized, though, that seeing Winona Marshall again might not be all that bad a thing, even if she was a Choctaw.

The longer he rode, the more intriguing that thought became. It was still difficult for him to realize that she was an Indian, since she didn't look—or act—like most other Indians he had encountered. He had to keep reminding himself that she was. Especially since he had come to know in the past few days of traveling that there would never be anything permanent between him and Irene. Not that he had ever really thought there would be. But she had. That much was apparent. That, in turn, made him skittish about spending much more time in Cross River. The more he did, the more he might be seduced into staying around Cross River a little longer and a little longer. Then when he left Irene, it would be all the more difficult on both of them.

The days of traveling made all that clear to him, but such ponderings made it harder to keep Winona out of his thoughts. Without thoughts of Irene to really replace thoughts of Winona, the young Choctaw woman kept worming her way into his mind. He would let the thoughts run for a while every now and then, but mostly he fought them.

Less than a day after he had turned west, Calhoun spotted a cloud of dust in the distance. He stopped and watched it for a while, but it didn't seem to be moving very far or very fast. He angled toward it, moving slowly northwest, senses alert.

The cloud of dust came and went as the wind pushed it hither and yon periodically. Still, whenever the dust was visible, it seemed to him that he was getting closer to it.

He rode into a wide, deep, grassy gully. When he came up on the other side, a small herd of horses was almost on him. He pulled to the side, along the lip of the gully a little and turned to watch as the horses moved slowly past him.

Reading the brands was almost impossible, but he managed to catch sight of the Butterfield brand on at least two of the animals. Then, through the heavy, choking dust, he spotted several men pushing the horses along. They were vague figures, hard to see through the dust, but he did not think they were Indians. Not Comanches anyway. They didn't sound much like Indians either, with their hoarse curses and high-pitched, piercing whistles.

Whether they were Comanche, Choctaw, Chickasaw, or white, though, they had obviously stolen horses and seemed to be in a place they had no business being.

Calhoun pulled one of the Colt Walkers from a saddle holster and fired through the haze, emptying the revolver. He thought he saw one of the men fall from his mount, but he could not be sure. He put the pistol away and pulled out the other one.

Then the horses were past him, gone down into the gully, though the dust lingered, swirling a little in the breeze. Calhoun could no longer see any of the men, so he rode the way the men had come from. Once he was beyond most of the dust, he cut through the lingering cloud.

Then something punched him hard high up on the back of the left shoulder and then another in the lower left ribs from the front. He heard two gunshots as he fell off the bay horse.

Some moments later, he was dimly aware of a man on a horse looking down at him. He thought the man was pointing a revolver at him, and he figured he was about to die. He didn't regret it; indeed, he looked forward to it. With death, he would join his beloved Lizbeth and Lottie. That was a pleasing thought.

The man on the horse suddenly disappeared, shouting something about the horse with the fancy saddle.

By then, though, Calhoun no longer cared about anything of this world, since blackness had swept over him like fast-building storm clouds over the plains.

Calhoun figured he had gone to hell, since when he opened his eyes there was an Indian's face looming over him. He shut his eyes again and groaned at his misfortune. After all those years of hoping to die so he could be with Lizbeth and Lottie again, he had been so sinful that he had died and been sent to hell, there to live in eternity with red-skinned savages his only companions.

Calhoun, who was afraid of nothing in heaven or hell—or on earth—bravely opened his eyes again. There was another Indian face hanging only a couple feet above him. This one, though, was not so unbearable to look at. It was mighty familiar, too, and it took him a moment to realize it was Winona Marshall.

"I ain't dead?" he croaked.

"No," Winona said with a worried smile.

"Good." Calhoun drifted into unconsciousness again. The next time he awoke, he knew where he was immediately, but he wasn't sure how he felt about it. The thought of being in the Choctaw town was unsettling and annoying. He didn't know what kind of strange things they had been doing to him in the name of doctoring him. Besides, feeling the way he did about Indians, he would much rather be with his own kind. Then he shook his head in anger, remembering that his own kind had been the ones to put him in this condition.

"How're you feelin'?" Winona asked quietly.

Calhoun realized it was the second or third time she had asked. "Fine," he said, voice rusty.

"Hungry?"

Calhoun shrugged, and then clamped his eyes and mouth tight against the wave of pain that ripped from the shoulder wound and spread throughout his torso. When the pain had subsided some, he opened his eyes again. "Water first," he said.

Winona left and came back a moment later with her father and a tin cup filled with water. Marshall held Calhoun's head up while Winona held the cup for him.

Calhoun drank greedily, heedless of all the water that splattered his chin and chest. Finally he had had enough, and Marshall eased him down.

"Hungry now?" Winona asked.

"Yes." His voice sounded more normal this time.

He ate some broth then, neither knowing nor caring who had made it or what was in it. It tasted good and seemed to send strength roaring through his veins.

* * *

Calhoun recovered fairly quickly, though it still took some weeks. He improved a little each day for a week or so, then relapsed into fever and delirium. Once that had passed, Calhoun made rapid progress, though Winona, her father, and her grandfather would not let him try too much at any one time.

Calhoun learned early on that he had been unconscious for more than a week and, despite his swift progress, he still was feeling quite weak a month after getting shot. In another two weeks, though, he was almost back to himself. It was deep in the summer now, with the temperatures hot and the humidity up. Between the lingering pain of his wounds, his annoyance at being stuck in an Indian village, and his anger at his predicament in general, he was a foul-humored man these days.

Nearly seven weeks after Calhoun had been shot, Jackson came into the room with a bottle of whiskey in one hand and two tin mugs in the other. He sat in one of the two chairs at the table nearby. "Join me," he said.

When Calhoun sat, Jackson held up the bottle. "The downfall of a great many people, Mister Calhoun."

Calhoun nodded. There was nothing to say to that.

"Makes you crazy to have an Indian with a bottle of whiskey, don't it?" There was no humor in his voice.

Calhoun nodded again.

"Well, Mister Calhoun, this here bottle is gonna help us have a little talk."

"Don't count on it, Chief." He was only a little sarcastic.

Jackson filled the mugs and set the bottle down. He lifted his cup. "Drink up, Mister Calhoun."

Calhoun shrugged and swallowed some whiskey. It wasn't very good, but it still snaked a warm trail down into his insides. He appreciated that.

Over the next several hours, the two men worked steadily at reducing the contents of the bottle. When they had accomplished that task, Jackson called for another. As she had been every time she had come in to bring the men food, Winona was tight-lipped, her eyes snapping in fury, as she brought in a fresh bottle of whiskey. She was angry and disgusted with both Calhoun and her grandfather.

Well on their way to having a good drunk, Jackson finally asked, "Do you believe me now when I tell you that white men are stealing the stage company's horses and mules?"

Calhoun shook his head. He was far less drunk than Jackson was, and more in control of himself.

"Who shot you?"

"White men."

"Any of these men the ones?" Jackson asked, spreading out some papers on the table and pushing them toward Calhoun.

Calhoun looked with bleary eyes at the papers. None meant anything to him but one. He gazed down at the drawing and had the ghostly remembrance of a face way above him, behind a pistol aimed at his head. Calhoun stabbed the piece of paper with a forefinger. "He was there."

"That's Micah Alexander," Jackson said. "I'd bet the horses were Butterfield ones, too." Jackson's words were slurred some, but he still seemed to be speaking well.

"I saw a couple that were."

"Horse thieves hit the station near Kiamichi three days before you were shot."

"These were comin' from the northeast," Calhoun said.

Jackson nodded, and then took several seconds to stop the room from spinning. Then he picked up another of the papers. Holding it so Calhoun could see the picture, he said, "We found this man dead, not far from where we found you."

Calhoun shrugged, not caring. He poured more whiskey down his gullet, hoping it would knock him out, or dull his senses, so he would no longer have to sit here and have his age-old hatreds ravaged to make him see the truth.

"He's one of Alexander's men. Has been for years," Jackson said.

"Too goddamn bad, Chief," Calhoun snapped.

"What's too goddamn bad is that you can't see what's real," Jackson said every bit as harshly as Calhoun had spoken. "What the hell's in your past that you'd hate my people—ones who've never done you any harm, only help—so much?" he demanded, voice rising in anger.

"None of your goddamn business, Chief," Calhoun snarled. "Have another goddamn drink and stop trying to make me a goddamn Indian lover, you red-skinned son of a bitch."

Another two hours—two silent hours—later, both men were very drunk. It was that reason, and that reason only, that made Calhoun open up to the old Choctaw, who seemed to sober up a little as he listened.

In short, clipped, hate-drenched sentences, Calhoun explained about Lizbeth and Lottie. About the farmstead in Kansas Territory. About how he had been gone, scouting for the army out in Wyoming Territory, leaving his wife and their infant child alone. No matter that he was on the way home. About the raid by the Sioux that left everything he had ever loved a shambles. About the broken bodies he found. About the piles of smoldering ashes where his house, his home, had been. About the blood-soaked ground around the focal point of the devastation.

The hate grew, swelling in the heat of Calhoun's passions. As his anger rose, his voice grew more bitter and sharp. Expletives dotted his speech, and then overtook it, as his words twisted with the bile that swept up his throat and threatened to choke him.

Then there were no more words; only feelings. The absolute sense of loss and alienation. The depth of his loathing for all Indian peoples. The sickness of the guilt that squeezed his heart. The breadth of his self-hatred. And the all-encompassing desire to die at last to join his Lizbeth and Lottie. Then, and only then, could he beg their forgiveness for having deserted them when they had needed him most.

Unconsciously, his hand reached for one of his Dragoons. He would end it all here and now, himself. Then he would be free of these demons. *But where are my pistols?* he wondered in anger. *They're always with me, the only tools of my survival, the preferred tools of my own destruction.*

"What's wrong with him, Grandfather?" Winona asked in shock. She had just come into the room to see if she could get the two men anything. She was shocked by the look on Calhoun's face.

"Nothing," Jackson mumbled.

"Hogwash," Winona screeched. "What have you done to him, Grandfather?"

Jackson lurched to his feet. "Never mind that. Just help me get him to bed, Granddaughter," he said, words slurred.

CHAPTER
∗ 16 ∗

Calhoun awoke the next morning with a crushing hangover. He remembered little of the latter parts of the night. Nor could he remember a time when he had gotten so drunk. He didn't think he ever had.

He groaned when he stood. Pain lanced through his shoulder and his head and his stomach recoiled with the remains of last night's foul brew. He managed to keep down the threatening eruption of vomit, but only with a massive dose of willpower.

When the first pangs of the hangover subsided a little, he staggered toward the door. He needed coffee. As he came to the table, he stopped. Seeing the drawings of Micah Alexander and his men brought back at least some of his and Jackson's conversation about the outlaw. Right now, though, Calhoun decided he did not care.

He managed to make the door and get it open. Several of the Choctaws were sitting at the table across the wide room. They looked at him and nodded.

Winona got one glimpse of him and rushed to him, scowling darkly at her grandfather as she did. She grabbed Calhoun and helped him back into the room and the bed. "What do you want?" she asked.

"Coffee?"

"You stay right here," Winona ordered. "I'll be right back." She was true to her word and soon returned with a small coffeepot and a mug. She filled the mug and put the pot on the table. She helped him gulp down some coffee.

"There any whiskey left in that bottle?" he asked, grinding his teeth to keep from vomiting.

"Looks like a little," Winona said after a glance at the table. "Why?"

"Get it."

"No," Winona said indignantly.

"Get it," Calhoun snarled.

Winona was shaken a little by his tone, but she got up and got the bottle.

Calhoun grabbed it and swallowed down the two mouthfuls or so that were left in the bottom. They went a fair way toward settling his stomach. "Thanks," he said with a grimace. He held out the bottle. When Winona took it, he asked politely, "More coffee, please."

Winona nodded, took his cup, and walked to the table. She put the empty whiskey bottle down and filled the coffee cup. Once again she helped him drink. "Hungry?" Winona asked when he had finished that cup of coffee.

Calhoun shook his head, very gently. "More sleep," he mumbled. He slid under the covers and was asleep in moments.

He awoke late in the night. He felt considerably better. He shuffled quietly out to the kitchen and rustled himself up some bacon and beans, plus some coffee, all the while trying not to wake Jackson and his wife, who were sleeping in the sitting area.

He ate in "his" room for the same reason. After eating, he smoked and sipped at coffee. For a while he paced the room, but then he realized that he was just avoiding what he knew he had to do. Finally he went to the table and looked at the drawings, each identified with a name scrawled at the bottom. He was sure now that Micah Alexander had been the one who had looked down from the horse at him while he lay there wounded.

Standing there, Calhoun picked up the paper with the face of the man who had been found dead at the scene of the short gun battle. After looking at it for some moments, he released it and watched it flutter back to the tabletop. There was no denying it any longer—he had to accept the fact that Alexander and his gang of men were the ones responsible for the horse thefts, not the Comanches or the Choctaws.

Once he had made the decision, accepting it as the right thing, he could more easily plan what he would do. Not that he could actually plan anything. But he knew that as soon as he was able, he would ride back to Cross River and report to Ferguson. That done, he could change his searching now that he knew he would be looking for white men. He could take these drawings with him and show them wherever he went. Someone somewhere would have seen the gang or knew where its members generally hid out. His search would be ever so much easier.

It took him a couple of days to get fully used to the idea, as well as to calm himself. He was eager to be away, hunting down the men who had tried to kill him, but he was not ready for that. As much as he might want to do that, he was physically not yet quite capable. He knew, though, that it would not be long before he was.

"Where're you going, Granddaughter?" Jackson asked Winona two nights later.

"To his room, Grandfather," Winona said bluntly, speaking, as had her grandfather, in Choctaw.

"Come, child and sit," he said. "I've got to talk to you."

Winona cast a longing glance at Calhoun's door, then sat next to her grandfather.

"He hates Indians, you know," Jackson said. "All Indians. Doesn't matter what kind."

"I'll change his thinking," Winona said confidently.

"I don't think so." Jackson paused. Looking into his granddaughter's eyes, he said, "He'll kill me, I think, if he learns that I've told you or anyone else." He grinned a little. "But I'm an old man, and death doesn't frighten me."

"Stop talking about your death, Grandfather."

Jackson smiled again. Then he explained as much of Calhoun's history concerning Indians as he could remember from that drunken night.

When Jackson had finished, Winona nodded solemnly. Then she stood. "I'll go to him now, Grandfather," she said simply. "I'll get him to accept me. And all of us."

"But what . . . ?" Jackson stopped and shook his head. He feared for her, not wanting to see her crushed by Calhoun's rejection. But Winona was eighteen and thought she could do anything. He could not turn her away from this course, and so he would not even try. "I hope so, Granddaughter," he said quietly.

Winona smiled and touched a finger to one of Jackson's

old, wrinkled cheeks. Then she turned and walked to Calhoun's room. She stopped at the door to collect herself, then eased the door open.

Calhoun, who had not yet fallen asleep, though he was in bed, asked, "Who's there?" His hand absently searched for one of his pistols.

"Winona." She came into the room and shut the door.

"What're you doin' here at this hour?" Calhoun asked. He did not feel like being disturbed. It had rained that day, and his new wounds were aching, as were a few old ones.

"I come lookin' for you, Wade Calhoun."

Calhoun sat in the dark, wondering what Winona was up to.

Suddenly a match flared, and then a lantern was lit. Winona turned down the wick so the lantern threw only a small, flickering yellow light. Then she marched to the side of the bed. "I tried to thank you for helpin' me once before," she said. "You wouldn't let me. I won't be denied now."

"Go away, Winona," Calhoun said wearily.

"Don't you want me?"

"No," Calhoun said flatly.

"You afraid of women?"

Calhoun's eyebrows raised, but he said nothing, knowing such a question did not need an answer.

"Then what's the problem?"

Calhoun didn't really want to hurt Winona's feelings. She was, after all, a woman, and should be treated well. On the other hand, he figured that being rude was going to be the only way to get rid of her. "I hate you," he said bluntly.

"I don't believe you," Winona responded stubbornly. "I hate all Indians. I told you that before."

Winona bent a little and picked up one of Calhoun's hands and then placed it on one nightdress-covered breast. "Are you sure?" she asked, voice deepening.

"Yes," Calhoun lied.

"I don't believe you." She rubbed his unresisting hand in small circles on her breast. "Not all Indian people're the same, Mister . . . Wade," she said huskily. "I sometimes think the Choctaws're more white than Indian," she added, "what with all the years we've spent learnin' to live like the white man."

Calhoun suddenly decided that Winona Marshall was far more woman than she was Choctaw. She felt like a woman, looked like a woman, smelled like a woman. She didn't really feel like, look like or smell like an Indian. He gave her breast a little squeeze.

Winona looked down at Calhoun and smiled as he moved over in the bed a little. Winona tugged off her nightdress and dropped it on the floor. A moment later she was cuddled next to Calhoun, enjoying the manly hardness of his hands—and other parts—on her skin.

Two months to the day after he was shot, Calhoun rode out of Boggy Hollow. The last week he had stayed there were indelibly imprinted on his brain. Winona had spent every night with him after that first time.

The first morning after, he had wrestled with his conscience, berating himself silently for having succumbed to her feminine wiles and subjugating his well-deserved hatred of Indians. But as he walked around Boggy Hollow that day, he looked at the Choctaws.

They were, indeed, more like whites in many ways than Indians. Even worse, they still had all the Indians' problems with white men, while trying to be like white men.

Calhoun had stopped at one point, when he saw Winona come out of her grandfather's house. He watched as she walked down a lane. Even looking at her from fifty yards away, he could see her, smell her, feel her in his bed and in his arms.

"Dumb bastard," he mumbled. He was not in love with Winona Marshall. Never could be. But he was certainly taken with her as a woman, and there was no use fighting it. Once again, when his decision was made, the guilt left him.

A week later he began making plans to leave, bringing up another problem. "You got a horse I can buy from you, Chief Jackson?" he asked one afternoon as he took a seat next to the old Choctaw on a log bench outside the house. "When I got shot, my horse run off. I think those horse thieves took it."

"You believe that white men're the horse thieves now?" Jackson asked in some surprise.

"Yes," Calhoun said tightly, not wanting to talk about it. "You got a horse or not?"

"I expect we can find you one in Boggy Hollow," Jackson said dryly.

"Saddle and other tack, too?"

Jackson nodded. "That's right, you had that fancy Mexican saddle."

"Another reason for me to look for those bastards," Calhoun said angrily. Taking that saddle had taken all he had, really. He would get it back, or die in trying.

Jackson looked squarely at Calhoun. "I'd like to

send some of my young men with you after the thieves," he said.

Calhoun was about to turn Jackson down flat, but then he realized that with all Jackson and the Choctaws had done for him, Jackson deserved to be heard. "Why?"

"Catching—or killin'—those horse thieves'll make life easier for my people." He looked across his village. "You ain't the only one thinks we've had somethin' to do with all those horse thefts. I know damn well there're white men out there who'll use that as an excuse to pry more land from us."

"I understand, Sam," Calhoun said honestly. "But I can't have a bunch of Choctaws runnin' around down in Texas. That'd cause a hell of a lot more trouble than it'd solve."

Jackson nodded, accepting. "You'll let some of my men escort you back to Cross River?" he asked. Then he smiled. "After all, it's all Choctaw land."

"That it is." Calhoun sighed. "Agreed."

The same five Choctaws went with Calhoun this time, too. They rode southeast right off, heading directly for Colbert's Ferry. It took only a day.

Just before Calhoun went to ride on the ferry, Zachary Marshall stopped him. "I know you still don't care much for my people, Mister Calhoun, despite the time you've spent with my daughter, but I want to tell you this: if you need help, come to me or Chief Jackson. You'll do better than if you go to your own people."

Calhoun believed him. He nodded and shook hands with Marshall. "I'll keep that in mind." He mounted his horse and rode down to the ferry.

Calhoun figured out later that someone must have seen

him heading the short distance from the ferry landing to Cross River, since there were six armed men waiting in Ferguson's office with the stage line superintendent. One of them wore a badge. All looked decidedly unfriendly.

"Where the hell've you been, goddammit?" Ferguson stormed. He was not afraid of Calhoun since he had his gunmen right there.

"Recuperatin'," Calhoun said flatly. He hooked his thumbs into his gun belt, near his pistols.

"From what?"

"I found some of your goddamn horse thieves. A pack of wolves led by a man named Micah Alexander. Trouble was, there was a heap more of them than there was of me. I killed one of 'em—Jerry Schrier—but the others got me good."

"Where'd you recover?"

"Boggy Hollow. In the house of Chief Jackson."

"Bullshit," Ferguson said flatly. "You're in cahoots with the goddamn Indians, stealin' Butterfield horses and selling them to the goddamn Choctaws or Chickasaws, or maybe the goddamn Cherokees. But who you sell them to isn't important. Only that we know you're in cahoots with them."

"How do you know that?"

"You've been employed by me for three, almost four, months, and you haven't brought in one horse or horse thief. You left here two months ago with three days' of supplies, then waltz back in here two months later with some story about being saved by Choctaws—a people you hate, if I remember correctly."

Calhoun was about to protest, but he knew it would do no good. Ferguson had made up his mind.

"Arrest him, men," Ferguson said.

CHAPTER

✴ 17 ✴

The Cross River jail wasn't great, of course, but it was a lot better than some other jails Calhoun had been in. This one was at least free of larger vermin and rodents.

Calhoun had not resisted when he was arrested. Not in the face of six armed men just looking for an excuse to shoot him down. He was swiftly relieved of his two Colt Dragoons and the bowie knife. His jailers did not know about his backup weapon—the deadly, cut-down Colt Walker—or the dirk he kept in his boot. They would get him out of here sooner or later. But as he always had in such situations, he bided his time, waiting for the right opportunity.

Irene McGowan came to visit him the day he was arrested. It was fairly late in the afternoon when she bustled in ahead of the town marshal, Ike Lewis.

"But it ain't safe for me to let you in that cell with him, Miz McGowan," Lewis was protesting.

"Marshal," Irene said, stopping and turning to look at the lawman, "Mister Calhoun is not going to hurt me. Nor is he going to take me prisoner to gain his freedom. However, if he does that, you may shoot me down so you can get at him."

"Yes'm," Lewis said glumly.

"Besides, I know—I just know—that he is innocent of whatever charges that evil Mister Ferguson has concocted against him."

"Yes'm." Lewis was a tall, spare man, who looked older than he was. He appeared to have little energy even at the best of times, and to look at him, one would think he went through life asleep on his feet. He wasn't nearly as dopey as he looked, though. He went around Irene and unlocked the cell door. When Irene stepped inside, he locked it behind her. "You mind your manners, boy," he warned and left.

"What's this all about, Wade?" Irene demanded, letting her anger show.

He explained it in a couple of sentences. When he saw the skepticism on her face, he scowled. "That's the same reaction I got from Ferguson," he snapped. Then he sighed, calming himself. He unbuttoned his shirt halfway down, peeled it back over his shoulder and turned. After their intimacies, Calhoun figured Irene certainly would know a new wound on his body.

"Does it still hurt?" she asked.

He shook his head as he pulled the shirt up and turned. He buttoned the garment.

"Did Mister Ferguson see that?"

Calhoun shook his head. "He wouldn't believe his own eyes anyway."

"That's the problem, isn't it?" Irene asked, understanding. "He doesn't believe you."

Calhoun nodded.

"Why?"

"Don't know. I think it's more that he doesn't *want* to believe me. He doesn't want to believe that white men are behind the horse thefts. He'd rather blame it on Indians."

"So did you not so long ago."

"Yep," Calhoun acknowledged. "But I was the one who was shot by the thieves. I know they're white. And if the Choctaws hadn't of found me and took care of me, my bones'd be bleachin' now out there somewhere."

"This's big trouble," Irene said seriously. "What can I do to help, Wade?"

"The best thing you can do, Irene, is to keep your distance from me," Calhoun said bluntly.

"But I don't want to do that. I . . ."

"Just do what I say, Irene," Calhoun said flatly. "The more you're seen with me, the harder it's gonna go on you. Keep your distance."

"But what about us?" Irene asked, suddenly worried and very frightened.

"There won't be any us if Ferguson and the others have their way. They'll hold a quick trial, find me guilty, and sentence me to hang. They've got it all figured out. Believe me, I know."

"But what . . ." Irene was close to tears.

"Listen to me, Irene," Calhoun said harshly. "I don't figure to let them get away with it. I aim to get out of here."

"How?"

"I got ways. I don't know when I'll do it, but I don't want you anywhere around when I do. You act around town like you've had it with me. That way they won't come lookin' to bother you when I get out of here."

"I'll . . . I'll miss you."

Calhoun nodded.

"Will I ever see you again?" Her lower lip was trembling.

"I'll come back when I get this all cleared up," Calhoun said evenly. He really had no plans to do any such thing. Besides, there was a very good chance he wouldn't live long once he got out of here and tracked the outlaws down.

"You sure there's nothin' I can do?"

Calhoun nodded, then stopped. "Wait, maybe there is. The last time I saw Alvin, he thanked me for saving his hide from Talbot and Graham."

Irene nodded. "Yes, he's mentioned it to me several times."

"Tell him to buy my horse, saddle, and tack."

"That good saddle of yours?"

Calhoun shook his head. "No, the bay was stolen, with the saddle. This's a short, chesty pinto over at the livery. I got it from the Choctaws." He pulled out his last three double eagles. "Here," he said, handing them to Irene. "Tell him to use this."

Irene was about to refuse, but she couldn't. She did not have that kind of extra money, and she was sure Webb didn't either. She took it. "What then?"

"Have him saddle the horse every night about dusk and leave it in the fenced-in yard behind your boardinghouse. Have the saddlebags packed with enough food supplies to last a couple days. On his way to work each morning, tell him to look for the horse. If it's there, he can ride it to work and unsaddle it there. If it ain't there, you'll know I'm gone."

Irene nodded.

"That's as close to me as I want you to get until this's all over."

Irene nodded again, then called for the marshal. Moments later, she was outside and Lewis was locking the door again.

That night, Calhoun was lying on his bunk, puffing on a cigarette, when he heard someone calling him softly from outside. He stood and looked through the narrow, barred window.

"I bought your horse, Mister Calhoun," Webb said.

"Obliged."

"I'll do as you say with it. I owe you that much." He paused, then looked up defiantly. Calhoun could see in the moonlight that Webb's face was cleared of the bruises he had suffered. "But I'm warnin' you, Mister Calhoun, that when this's over, I aim to compete with you for Miss Irene."

"You like her that much, do you, boy?" Calhoun asked with a sneer.

"Yessir."

If Calhoun was a smiling man, he would've done so then. "We'll see what happens, boy."

Calhoun waited two more full days before he made his move. That way he had time to figure out when his meals would come and to plan accordingly. He could see the marshal's office through the door when old Mrs. Carson brought the meals, and he noted that it was almost always empty at those times. Lewis would come through the door, take a look at Calhoun, then come into the little hallway that ran in front of the three cells. Mrs. Carson would follow him. After unlocking the cell door, Lewis would watch Calhoun while Mrs. Carson entered and put the tray down.

On the third night of Calhoun being an inmate in the Cross River jail, Lewis came to the cell with Mrs. Carson as usual. This time he was grinning widely.

Calhoun said nothing, figuring that if Lewis was so

all-fired up with news, he'd spill it sooner or later. He did.

As he was locking the cell door after Mrs. Carson had walked out, Lewis said, "Your trial starts day after tomorrow. It's gonna be a short one, but gratifyin', I figure."

"Don't count on it," Calhoun said calmly. He did nothing that night, but he decided that he would take action the next evening.

Lewis made his way down the cell that next evening with Mrs. Carson behind him. The marshal was even whistling some little tune. It all annoyed Calhoun.

Calhoun sat on his cot as usual, but when Mrs. Carson was inside the cell, he stood, the cut-down Walker in his fist, cocked. "Step inside, Marshal," Calhoun ordered.

Lewis hesitated, figuring the odds. They were not good. Not good at all. He was not as good with a pistol as he had wanted to be and the weapon that Calhoun was holding looked mighty nasty from this angle. He nodded and stepped inside.

With his left hand, Calhoun grabbed Lewis's revolver. He uncocked the Walker and slid it away. Then, without apology or warning, he walloped Lewis on the back of the head with the butt of Lewis's own revolver. Lewis sank down half on the cot and half on the floor. Calhoun lifted Lewis's legs onto the cot. Then he turned to Mrs. Carson. "You got a choice, ma'am," he said quietly. "Promise me you'll keep quiet, or . . ." He wiggled the pistol butt.

"I should worry about that scoundrel?" she asked, pointing at Lewis.

Calhoun nodded. He went outside the cell and picked up the keys. He locked the door and then put the keys on the floor, far enough so that the short Mrs. Carson wouldn't be able to reach them, but near enough that, with a stretch, Lewis should be able to pull them in.

Calhoun walked swiftly to the office, closing the wood door to the cells behind him. It took only moments for him to locate his Colts, strap on the gun belt and then check the revolvers. He also found his bowie knife and slid that away. He shoved Lewis's pistol into the back of his gun belt. Then he went to the door and stood next to it, hidden by the wall, but able to see out the window in the door as well as the window in the wall to his right.

When it was fully dark, and Calhoun was sure no one was right in front of the office, he stepped outside and then headed down the street at a good pace. The pinto that Jackson had given Calhoun—not sold; the old chief would not hear of such a thing—was saddled and waiting in Irene's back yard. He patted the animal on the neck, once again cognizant of the irony. He had had a pinto when this latest adventure had started, and here he had another one. He hoped this one fared better than the last.

Calhoun glanced up at Irene's window but did not see her. He was just as glad. He pulled himself into the saddle and rode to the gate. He opened it and moments later closed it without dismounting. He trotted east out of Cross River, then cut north to the river. He swam the horse across the Red, knowing he was taking a risk by not using the ferry, but that was out of the question.

On the river's north bank, he swung west and rode hard until he cut the stage road. He slapped the horse into a run, heading northeast up the road. After half an hour, he slowed the horse, but kept a steady, strong pace. He rode straight on through the next day before finally pulling off the road a little way.

His camp that night was a poor one, since he didn't want to start a fire this close to the stage road. He was also bone tired, and performed his chores only because they had to be done. He did sleep long and well, though, waking shortly after dawn.

Deciding that no one would be able to see a fire in the daylight, especially behind the screen of brush, he built one and then ate a hot meal. It wasn't the most filling meal he'd ever had, but it was hot and relatively tasty.

Done, he began to hurry, wanting to be on the trail. He was eager to catch the outlaws. Soon he was on the road again. He cut left at about the same spot he had the last time. When he got to the gully where he had been shot, he turned southward, figuring the outlaws had been going that way for some reason. Calhoun hoped they had a hideout down that way. If they did, he would find it.

Darkness was falling, though, so he stopped. Once again he opted not to have a fire. After tending to the horse and eating some jerky, Calhoun walked in a circle around his camp, spending the most time on the southern arc. He hoped to spot a fire or other sign that man—particularly the outlaws—was around. He saw nothing.

He made a fire in the morning, ate quickly, and got back on the move. He rode slowly but steadily through the many gullies and over the many grassy ridges. There were plenty of places a man or two could've hidden—thickets, groves of elms and chinaberries—but nothing that would hide half a dozen or more outlaws plus a couple dozen horses.

Calhoun had been a scout for a long time and had acquired skills he had never forgotten, and ones he didn't know he had half the time. He wasn't sure what stopped him, or what made him look to the west, but he did. He began to think he was going *loco*, when he spotted a wisp of smoke. He nodded to himself and turned in that direction.

When he made camp that night, it was again a cold camp. In the darkness, he walked around it as he had the night before. He saw nothing, which meant to him that whoever had produced that smoke a little earlier must be in a deep gully or a canyon. He went to sleep with the knowledge that his search might be over very, very soon.

He found the mouth of a small canyon after only an hour's ride the next morning. The ground had been pretty well beat up, signifying that a heap of horses had come this way. As he rode cautiously into the canyon, he had the feeling that he was in a hollow back in Tennessee. Trees and brush were thick in spots, yet there were meadowlike spots scattered around.

As soon as he spotted several canvas tents, he ducked into the brush just to his left. He dismounted and walked along, tugging the horse with him. He stopped before the brush thinned too much, tied the pinto to a small elm, and then moved up as close to the edge of the brush as he dared and squatted.

It took him less than a minute to spot Micah Alexander.

CHAPTER

* 18 *

Calhoun counted eight men in the camp, living in three tents. He estimated there were three dozen horses grazing in the vicinity. From the drawings old Sam Jackson had shown him, he could pick out all the men in the camp. Besides Alexander, there was Pat Bayless, Bob Gaines, Tom Duncan, Dick Isaacson, Art Nash, Mike Duffy, and Chris Wilde.

Wilde was squatting at the fire in front of the center tent casting lead balls. Duffy and Duncan were sitting on a log near the tent on Calhoun's right. They were drinking coffee and talking idly. Alexander was wandering through the horses, checking them over. Isaacson, Bayless, and Nash were with him. Gaines was sitting on a rock by the other tent, cursing as he tried to darn a shirt.

Calhoun decided there was no real reason to wait. He checked the pistol he had taken from Marshal Lewis back in Cross River and returned it to his belt. Then he checked his two Colt Dragoons. With the latter revolvers in hand, he stood and strode out into the open.

Duncan and Duffy never knew what hit them, as Calhoun drilled them smoothly and easily with the Colt in his right hand. Gaines, on the left, suffered the same fate from the spitting muzzle of Calhoun's other Dragoon.

Wilde looked up, frightened, and began trying to get his pistol out. Calhoun shot him in the gun arm, then in the other arm. When Wilde managed to get to his feet, Calhoun shot him in a leg.

Alexander was fast, Calhoun had to admit that. Before Calhoun had fired his half dozen shots, Alexander was on a horse and riding like hell, pushing most of the herd before him toward the mouth of the canyon. Isaacson, Nash, and Bayless were right behind him, driving the rest of the horses. Within a minute, they were just dots bobbing on the horizon, and soon after even the sound of the horses' drumming hooves was gone.

Calhoun dropped one Colt into his holster and began loading the other one as he walked toward the tents. Keeping a wary eye on Wilde, he checked Duncan and Duffy. Both were dead. Calhoun finished loading the one revolver, holstered it, and began reloading the other. He walked near to Wilde, who was moaning, on his way to make sure Gaines also was dead.

Then he strolled back to Wilde and squatted next to him. "Talk," he ordered.

"About what?"

Calhoun grabbed Wilde's left arm and twisted it.

Wilde screamed and his face turned pasty white as the ends of the bone broken by Calhoun's bullet grated together.

"Talk," Calhoun said again.

"Where should I start?" Wilde responded quickly.

"How do the horse thefts work?"

"Alexander picks a target, then rounds us up. We hit the place at night, nice and quiet, and run off all the stock we can. We usually ride up here and set a few days. Then, while we watch over the stock, Alexander goes out and sells the horses. When he gets back, we deliver."

"Who buys most of 'em?"

"Injins. Cherokees mostly, but the Choctaws and the Chickasaws also do. All the Injins sell 'em back to white folks somewhere. Sometimes to the army, sometimes even back to the Butterfield company. But they'll sell 'em to anyone who comes along." Wilde spit, but that did nothing to ease his pain. "Jesus, mister, did you have to shoot me three times?" he asked plaintively.

"Yep. Why do the Indians buy 'em? They've got to know they're stolen animals."

"Hell, everyone thinks the damned Injins're stealin' 'em anyway. They don't give a shit. They figured that what the hell, if they're gonna git blamed for it, they might's well make themselves a few bucks on it."

Calhoun nodded. "How's Alexander know where to raid?"

Wilde shrugged and realized straight off that that was a bad move. "I ain't sure. I know he's got one feller works for the company feedin' him information."

"Who?"

"Templeton."

"Will Templeton?" Calhoun asked surprised.

"No, the kid. What's his name?"

"Dewey."

"Yeah, that's it. The little bastard hates his old man, so he arranges—I don't know how—to have us boys hit his place, plus the one down on Denton Creek and a couple others, regularly."

Calhoun sat silently for a little, trying to digest the surprising piece of information. "How many men usually ride with Alexander?" he finally asked.

"This was the usual bunch, but Micah knows fellers from Mexico to Missouri he can call on when he needs help. He could probably put together a small army was the need to arise."

"Where's Alexander gonna go from here?"

Wilde didn't answer for a time, since he was lying there with his face all scrunched up in pain from his wounds. Then he finally said, "I ain't sure. There's a cave northeast of here, up on the western side of the Sans Bois Mountains."

"What's he plannin' next?"

"I don't know that either, but I figure it's somethin' big."

"Why?"

"He was supposed to meet a bunch of boys from Missouri and Arkansas soon. I don't know where or when for sure."

"How many's a bunch?"

"Don't . . . know." Wilde's voice was growing faint. He had lost a fair amount of blood and was weakening. Plus he was nearly unconscious from the pain. "Dozen maybe."

That many men, plus the three Alexander still had with him, could cause a fair amount of havoc on a far-flung, mostly empty frontier. That, however, was not really his problem. Not directly. He wanted to catch Alexander and bring him back to Cross River. Or kill him. That would end it as far as Calhoun was concerned. However, if he ran into Alexander's new army, he would do what he could to cut it down to size.

"Kill me, mister," Wilde pleaded. "I don't . . . don't . . . want to bleed to death."

Calhoun shrugged and stood. He went into the center tent, figuring that to be Alexander's. He nodded in satisfaction when he spotted his saddle. He carried it outside and looked it over. It was dusty but otherwise in good shape. His rifle and shotgun were still in the scabbards, and the one Walker was still in the saddle holster. It was unloaded and had not been cleaned, Calhoun supposed from the look of it, since he had fired it that day against Alexander's men when he was wounded.

He set the saddle just inside the tent and then went to get the pinto. When he got back, Wilde was alive but unconscious.

Calhoun pulled the saddle he had gotten from Jackson off the pinto, and put his own saddle on the horse. He got his other Walker from the saddlebags he had just taken off the pinto. Then he cleaned and reloaded both Dragoons and both Walkers, taking his time.

Done with that, he took a few minutes to gobble down some corn bread and bacon, got some supplies and put them in his saddlebags. Finally he mounted the pinto, settling his rear end comfortably into the old, familiar saddle. Micah Alexander still had some things to pay for, but Calhoun figured he had evened up one small debt in getting the saddle back. Calhoun glanced at Wilde, who was still unconscious but breathing. Then Calhoun tugged on the horse and rode off.

It was dark before he hit the stage road, and so he stopped and made himself a cold camp. There was no telling where Alexander and his men were. He did not need to give himself away with a fire.

That became his pattern over the next several days, as he hunted Micah Alexander. He would build no fires at night, instead subsisting on jerky and water. He would have a fire in the mornings, make a small, hot breakfast and a small pot of coffee before packing up and riding on.

It was two full days' ride up the stage road before he was ready to cut east toward the rocky bulge of the Sans Bois on the horizon. Along the road on the second day, Calhoun pulled to the side when he saw the stage coming.

The coach was well past him before Frank Osgood realized who had been on the side of the road. The driver pulled the coach to a frantic stop as soon as he could. "Jumpin' sweet Jesus," Osgood said when Calhoun trotted up to the stage. "Where the hell'd you come from, Calhoun? Last I heard down in Cross River, everyone thought you'd skedaddled for good."

"Ran into the horse thieves, and . . ." He stopped to look at a passenger, who had stuck his head out the window.

"Is this a robbery, driver?" the passenger asked.

"No, Mister Fairchild," Osgood answered, "this is not a robbery."

"Then let's get movin', my good man. Some of us have business to see to, and standing here in the middle of the road talking with such a scoundrelish-looking fellow is not helping matters."

"He ain't a scoundrel, Mister Fairchild," Osgood said. "He works with us."

"Cleaning privies, I assume?" Fairchild said sarcastically.

Hard of face, Calhoun dismounted and handed his

reins to Osgood, who grinned. He was about to get a show, and he knew it.

Calhoun walked to the coach and pulled open the door even as Fairchild tried to shrink back inside. He reached inside, grabbed a handful of Fairchild's suit and hauled him out. Calhoun pointed to a nearby rock. "Sit," he commanded.

Fairchild looked up at Osgood, and then to Joel Hawthorn, his eyes asking them to interfere, to stop this madman from whatever it was he was about to do.

"I'd sit my ass down on that rock was I you, Mister Fairchild," Hawthorn said with a chuckle. "'Course, that's only my feelin's in the matter. You might feel some different about it all."

Fairchild slinked over to the rock and sat. His chubby face was red and coated with sweat. He looked decidedly nervous.

Calhoun mounted his horse again. "You were sayin'?" Osgood prompted as he handed the reins back. He was a little disappointed, since the entertainment hadn't been as good as he had expected.

"I ran into them horse thieves and we had us a little set-to. I got one of 'em, but they hit me twice. Next thing I knew I woke up in a Choctaw house over in Boggy Hollow."

"You're one lucky son of a bitch to have lived through bein' shot twice by Comanches."

"The thieves ain't Comanches."

"No?" Hawthorn asked, surprised.

"Nope. Whites. Micah Alexander's the leader."

"I've heard of him," Hawthorn agreed. "Mean bastard."

"What happened then?" Osgood asked.

"Took me two months to recover. When I got back

to Cross River, Ferguson went crazy. Accused me of bein' in cahoots with the thieves. Had Lewis throw me in jail." He nodded when four eyebrows facing in his direction went up in question. "I sat there a couple days, then decided I'd had enough. I knocked Lewis on the head and took off."

"Ferguson must be completely *loco* by now," Osgood said.

Calhoun shrugged. "I went out after Alexander's bunch. Found them over in a canyon north of Boggy Hollow. Killed four, but four others got away with all the horses they had there. One of the four I killed lived a while, and told me Alexander's got a hideout in some cave over in the Sans Bois."

Osgood nodded. "You be careful."

Calhoun shrugged. Neither danger nor death meant much to him.

"We'll keep quiet in Cross River about seein' you out here, Wade," Hawthorn said.

"Obliged."

"What about lard belly over there?" Osgood asked pointing to Fairchild.

"He been a pain in the ass the whole trip?"

"Right from the get-go."

"It's about time you put a good scare into him." Calhoun could see the interest in Osgood's eyes. "Ride off without him," he said.

"I can't do that!" Osgood said, shocked.

"Hell, you're not really gonna leave him here. Just ride off. Get a couple hundred yards down the road and stop. Let him come chasin' after you. You can tell him you forgot all about that he was sittin' there, and when you remembered, you stopped to wait for him."

"You're a devilishly sneaky bastard, Calhoun," Hawthorn said with a laugh. "Let's go, Frank."

The coach lurched off. Fairchild looked at it in disbelief. Then he leapt up. With a wary glance at Calhoun, he started waddling after the stage, hollering for it to stop.

Calhoun sat there on his horse shaking his head, watching. Finally Osgood stopped the coach and waited until Fairchild caught up. Calhoun figured the man was puffing like a steam engine. He turned his horse and rode on.

The next day, Calhoun pulled off the road, heading east for the low mountains. He stopped not far off, since dusk was hard upon him.

Calhoun spent three days searching the Sans Bois Mountains, looking for Alexander. He found the cave—at least he figured it was the cave, considering its size and the amount of usage it had gotten—on the third day. Though it did show plenty of signs of use, it had not been used any time recently. "Shit," Calhoun muttered as he looked out the cave mouth across the sweep of countryside.

Since the cave had some food supplies that still seemed edible, Calhoun stayed there that night. He enjoyed a hot supper for a change, and had plenty of coffee. Still, he did not get too comfortable. He had men to hunt, and he wanted to find them soon.

The next morning, he hit the stage road again, riding south at a good clip. He cut off the road two days later, heading for Boggy Hollow. He thought that perhaps the Choctaws had seen Alexander and his men.

A chill began gathering in the pit of his stomach as he neared the Choctaw village, and he was swept with a sense of doom. When he was only a mile away, he could see the smoke, far too much to be from cook fires. The smoke wafted through the trees and drifted lazily into the sky. The dread feeling increased and he urged the horse into a trot.

The scent of burned wood and pitch came to him, and his jaw tightened. Then he rode out from the trees onto what was—or had been—Boggy Hollow's main street. "Shit," he breathed. He galloped toward Jackson's house, fear and rage holding his heart hostage.

CHAPTER

* 19 *

Jackson's barn was burned to the ground, as was about half of his house. A goodly number of the other buildings in Boggy Hollow also were burned. Fields were trampled, but fortunately for the Choctaws, the bulk of their harvest had been in for a couple of weeks. Several bodies lay in the dirt streets, and dead cattle and hogs were scattered all over. Smoke still rose into the wind from the smoldering piles of ashes around the village.

Calhoun stopped outside Jackson's house and dismounted. His fear and worry had been supplanted by the cold tightness of anger. He walked purposefully into the house. He found Winona and her father kneeling over a gray-haired figure on the sitting room floor.

"Shit," Calhoun mumbled as he squatted next to Winona and looked down at the seamed face of Chief Sam Winter Bear Jackson. The old man's countenance was serene in death; below, however, Jackson's shirt was soaked with blood.

Winona looked at Calhoun, her pained face coated with tears, her eyes red.

"Come on," Calhoun said to her, rising and helping her up, "there's nothin' you can do for him now." He led Winona outside the house and sat her down on the bench he had occupied with Jackson not so long ago. "What happened?" he asked.

"About a dozen men rode through here," Winona sniffled. "They shot anyone they saw and set many of the buildings on fire."

"Who?"

"White men."

"Do you know which white men?" Calhoun asked, trying to be patient despite having to extract every teeny bit of information from Winona laboriously.

"Micah Alexander and his men," Zachary Marshall said from behind Calhoun.

"You sure?" Calhoun asked, turning to look at Marshall.

Marshall nodded. "I've encountered that son of a bitch before." The Choctaw's face was hard and unforgiving.

"Why?" Calhoun wondered aloud.

Marshall shrugged. "You'd have to ask them, but it did seem like they had made Sam's house the target."

"Then what's all the rest of this?" Calhoun asked, waving his arm to encompass Boggy Hollow.

Marshall shrugged. "Such men don't worry about killin' Indians, Calhoun. You know that. And ravagin' a Choctaw village doesn't concern them much."

"It doesn't make any sense," Calhoun commented. "But that doesn't matter." He rose, face set. "You got some supplies I can buy, Zach?" he asked.

Marshall shook his head. "No." The single word was filled with hatred, and he scowled at Calhoun. For the first time since Calhoun had arrived minutes ago, Marshall thought about the fact that Calhoun was white.

"Why not? I need some supplies to go after the sons of bitches who did this."

"You ain't going nowhere," Marshall growled, pulling a pistol on Calhoun.

Winona gasped, but Calhoun calmly said, "What the hell's goin' on here, Marshall?"

"You ain't the only man can hate those different from him, Calhoun," Marshall snarled. "It'd be just like a white man to come sashayin' in here after his partners've raided here."

"You're *loco*," Calhoun said tightly. He had had just about enough of Zach Marshall. He could understand the man's grief, and even his rage, but not being the wrong target for that anger.

"I am?" Marshall spit. He thumbed back the hammer of the pistol. "We ain't had nothin' but trouble since you showed up here the first time. I finally figured out that you're one of them. If you know any prayers, Calhoun, best speak them now."

"Stop it!" Winona screamed. She stood and got between Calhoun and her father, her back brushing Calhoun's front.

"Get out of the way, daughter," Marshall ordered.

"No, Pa. Not until you start makin' some sense," Winona said defiantly.

"I am makin' sense," Marshall snapped, anger and hatred not lessened one iota.

"No, you're not." She paused. "You're as bad as Wade is," she pressed. "Ready to hate everyone who ain't like them because a couple of those people did somethin' to hurt you. You're just tryin' to get back at Wade for his hatin' us when he first came here, Pa. You ever think why he did?" she demanded.

"No," Marshall mumbled, hate still eating at him.

"Wade's wife and baby girl were killed by a war band of Sioux—our ancient friends, if Grandfather's stories are to be believed. So he hates all Indians. Now you want to hate all white men because of what Alexander's outlaws did here today."

"Where'd you learn that?" Calhoun demanded.

"Does it matter?" Winona asked, shrugging. She still looked at her father.

"You don't know what you're talkin' about, daughter," Marshall said, a note of uncertainty in his voice.

"Don't I? Don't I? Who shot and almost killed Wade that time a couple months ago?"

"I don't know."

"Yes you do." Winona's voice was high and scratchy with grief, fear, and anger. "You were with Grandfather when he found that outlaw Wade shot. You know he was one of Alexander's men."

"Maybe he and Calhoun had a fallin' out and they tried to kill each other."

"Do you really believe that, Pa?"

Marshall lifted his eyes from his daughter's face to glare at Calhoun. He had been so certain moments ago.

"Every minute you stand here, those sons of bitches are gettin' farther away," Calhoun said. "I maybe don't have as much reason to hate Alexander as you got, but I hate him all the same."

Marshall still wasn't sure.

"Make up your mind, Zach," Calhoun said flatly. "Either shoot me here and now, or sell me some supplies so I can go track down Alexander."

Marshall hesitated only a few moments. Then he uncocked the pistol and holstered it. "I ain't gonna shoot you—now. And I won't sell you any supplies."

Calhoun shrugged. "I'll make do."

"I'll give you the damn supplies. But," Marshall added pointedly, "some of us're goin' with you."

Calhoun was about to object, but then realized he had no right to deny the Choctaws coming. They had suffered far worse than he had, though he felt the loss of old Sam Jackson tremendously. No one had ever treated him the way Jackson had. "You doin' this because you want to avenge old Sam? Or because you don't trust me?"

"Both," Marshall said bluntly.

"If you're plannin' to back shoot me out there so you don't have to do it in front of your daughter, you might's well just go on and do it here and now."

"If I ever find out you did somethin' like that, Pa," Winona said. "I'll . . ."

"I said I don't trust you, Calhoun," Marshall said flatly. "I didn't say I was gonna double-cross you." He paused. "But if you are one of Alexander's men, you will regret it."

Calhoun shrugged. "I ain't worried."

"Then let's go."

"We're not takin' more than five men, though," Calhoun said.

Marshall grinned humorlessly and nodded. "Six of us ought to be enough to handle those bastards. And five'll do if necessary," he added pointedly.

Calhoun nodded. "When did they ride out?"

"Two, three hours ago," Marshall said. "It took old Sam almost that long to die."

The hatred in Marshall's voice was still strong, and Calhoun could plainly hear it. He didn't mind, though. His own hate was pretty well a part of him now.

* * *

"You know where to look for them, Calhoun?" Marshall asked as they mounted their horses twenty minutes later.

"Nope. But I think I know where we might be able to find out."

"Where?"

Calhoun was not listening; he was already galloping out of Boggy Hollow. Marshall and the four other Choctaws—George Franklin, the first Choctaw that Calhoun had met; Tom Grant, who was married to Jackson's other daughter; Ray Jefferson and Abe Johnson, both of whom had lost family members in Alexander's raid—hurried to catch up to him.

They were a closemouthed group when they made camp late that night. Calhoun knew none of the Choctaws trusted him. He felt the same about them.

They hit the Red River the next afternoon. This late in the summer, the water level was down considerably, which worried all of them. The river had too many patches of quicksand to take lightly. But they made it across without mishap.

"Not heading for Cross River, Calhoun?" Marshall asked, surprised when Calhoun kept going south instead of turning east.

Calhoun shook his head. Neither man slowed his horse.

"Why not?"

"I don't think they'll be there."

"We should check," Marshall insisted.

"I'll get arrested if I go back there. Ferguson thought I was in cahoots with your people in stealin' the horses, or at least buyin' 'em from the thieves."

Marshall could think of no reply to that, so he shut up and kept riding.

The next afternoon, Calhoun slowed up, knowing he was getting near to Templeton's station. He cut southwest a little, and finally stopped when he came to Clear Creek. He dismounted. "We'll wait here for night," he said.

"Why?" Franklin asked.

"The station I need to go to is over yonder a half mile or so," Calhoun answered, pointing.

"So?"

"There ain't a lick of cover around it. You think the station master's going see five men he doesn't know, at least from a distance, and invite 'em in?"

"Suppose not," Franklin said. "Do we leave as soon as it's dark?"

"I," Calhoun responded, emphasizing the word, "will leave just before dark."

"We're coming with you," Marshall said from where he was unsaddling his horse. "I ain't about to let you just go ridin' off into the night."

Calhoun considered shooting Marshall, and then trying to get the rest of the Choctaws before they got him. He was tired of being issued orders. He knew, however, that such a thing would be plumb foolish. "Pick one of your men to go with me. The rest'll stay here," he countered, his voice indicating that he would brook no argument about it.

Marshall hesitated only a moment, then nodded. "I'll go."

They tended their horses, ate, and rested while they waited for night. As dusk was really taking hold, Calhoun rose and began saddling his horse. Marshall saw it and hurried to do the same. Without waiting for Marshall to finish, Calhoun mounted up and rode off. Marshall caught up to him right off.

It was dark when they spotted the light spilling from the cracks in Templeton's station. Calhoun's stomach recoiled as he thought of the fare Elva Templeton ladled out to the unsuspecting stage passengers unfortunate enough to stop there. He quickly pushed that thought out of his mind.

Calhoun dismounted and tied his reins to the pinto's foreleg. Marshall followed suit. Then the two began walking toward the house, Calhoun keeping them away from a direct line with the front door. Rex began barking as the two neared the house.

"Who's there?" Templeton bellowed from inside.

"It's Wade Calhoun. Open up!"

The door opened to reveal Templeton standing there with a rifle in his hands. Templeton sighed with relief. "Come on in, Mister Calhoun," he said.

Calhoun did, grabbed the rifle barrel and jerked the weapon out of Templeton's hand. "Come on in, Zach," he said.

Marshall, who had been waiting beside the door so he would not be seen, stepped inside, face hard. He had a revolver in his hand, and he pointed it at Rex, who was barking like crazy as Dewey Templeton held him.

"What the hell's this all about, Calhoun?" Templeton asked, voice suddenly gone harsh.

"Close the door, Elva," Calhoun ordered. He looked at Dewey. "Let the dog go, boy." Rex bounded over to Calhoun, who squatted and petted the animal. Then he let Rex get used to Marshall a little. Finally he rose.

"I asked you what the hell this was all about, Calhoun," Templeton said again. He did not like being ignored. He did not like men coming in and taking over his station house. He did not like Indians under his roof. In fact, there wasn't anything he liked about this situation.

"I need to have a talk with Dewey," Calhoun said flatly.

"What about?" Dewey asked, eyes wide.

"Watch him, Zach," Calhoun said, pointing to Templeton. He strolled over to where Dewey was sitting. "How long've you been workin' for Alexander?" he asked harshly.

"What the hell kind of question is that?" Templeton bellowed angrily.

"Zach, if he opens his trap again, slam it shut for him," Calhoun commanded without looking that way.

"With pleasure," Marshall responded. His hatred for white men was still running strong, and he would not mind taking it out on this white man, especially if he, or his son, might have something to do with Alexander.

"Dewey," Calhoun said slowly, "listen and listen good. You can do this the easy way. Or not. You answer my questions straight off, and you'll be fine. You give me a hard time and you'll experience pain. Lots of pain."

"I don't know what you're talkin' about," Dewey said nervously.

"Chris Wilde told me about you. Just before he died. Now, how long've you been workin' for Alexander?"

Dewey shook his head.

Calhoun sighed. "Get up," he ordered.

"What're you gonna do with me?" Dewey asked, frightened.

"Get up!" Calhoun roared. When Dewey stood, Calhoun grabbed him by the shoulder and shoved him toward the door. He looked at Elva. "I'm takin' your son out to talk to him, ma'am. I don't think it's somethin' you should see."

"I'm comin'," Templeton snapped.

Marshall was about to clout Templeton, but Calhoun stopped him. "He can come. I want him to hear what his son has to say." He turned back to Dewey and shoved him. "Move."

CHAPTER

* 20 *

At Calhoun's urging, Dewey sat on the ground in the Choctaws' camp. A fire of buffalo chips was hastily made. When its flames cast their light, Dewey looked around, and he did not like what he saw. Five of the six men, including the one who had come to the house with Calhoun, were dressed like white men, but they sure had the look of Indians about them, as far as he was concerned. He looked at his father, who was sitting not far away with two Choctaws standing over him. Templeton shrugged, but he looked worried.

Calhoun squatted across the fire from Dewey. "We're short on time, boy," he said harshly. "So I'd be obliged if you were to talk to me."

"I don't know what you want to know."

Calhoun sighed and rose. He stepped across the fire and kicked Dewey in the face.

Dewey yelped and fell onto his back. Calhoun was on him in an instant and dragged him up by the throat. With a kick Calhoun swept Dewey's feet out from under him. Dewey went down, face first this time, but Calhoun would not let his head hit the ground. Still holding him by the throat, Calhoun dragged Dewey to the fire, and held Dewey's face several inches above the flames, ignoring the fact that his own hands were there, too.

"Tell me about Alexander," Calhoun said harshly.

Dewey mumbled but really didn't say anything.

Calhoun shoved the young man's face closer to the fire. Still no response. Calhoun pushed Dewey's face almost into the coals.

Dewey screamed something unintelligible, then cried out, "I'll talk, dammit! I'll talk!"

Calhoun pulled him away from the fire and threw him to the ground. "Speak up, boy," he commanded. "Now!"

"I met Alexander a couple years ago down in Sharp Bend. I . . . well, I . . . wanted to join his gang when I heard about them. He offered me a way to do it." Dewey paused to sit up and touch his face. It felt warm to him, but otherwise all right. "I was to get word to him when I thought a station had new horses or some-thin'."

"How did you get word to him?" Calhoun asked, squatting across the fire from Dewey again.

"Sent a note." He looked into Calhoun's burning eyes. "With Charlie Endicott," he added hastily.

"The stage driver?" Calhoun asked, a little sur-prised. "He's in on all this, too?"

Dewey nodded.

"How about Waverly?"

Dewey shook his head. "Nope. He don't know noth-in' about any of this."

"How much is your cut?" Calhoun asked.

"Who cares, Calhoun?" Marshall snapped.

Calhoun looked at the Choctaw and nodded. "Where's Alexander and his men now?" he asked.

"They'll kill me if I tell you," Dewey whined.

"You don't think I will?" Calhoun demanded.

Dewey shrugged, scared to death.

"Well, I won't," Calhoun said evenly, shocking just about everyone. "What I will do, though, is carve your old man up in front of you." Remembering that Wilde had said Dewey hated his father, Calhoun added, "And if that ain't enough, I'll gut your ma in front of you, too."

"You bastard," Dewey snarled. Then he remembered where he was and who he was addressing and he clapped his mouth shut.

Marshall walked up behind Dewey and kicked him in the back. "Where is he?" His voice was flat and harsh.

"Sharp Bend!" Dewey shouted. "All of 'em. I swear."

"Endicott there, too?" Calhoun asked.

Dewey shrugged. "He was, but he might be headin' back this way."

Calhoun sat pondering it all, wondering what to do about Dewey Templeton. He looked at the young man's father. "I'm gonna entrust Dewey to your care until we can get back through here, Templeton," he said. "You understand what he's been mixed up in here?"

Templeton nodded. "I'll see that he don't pull no more of this shit, that's for sure," he growled.

"One other thing you ought to know, Templeton."

"What's that?"

"Your son hates you. You best think of that when your back's turned to him."

Templeton was so shocked that he couldn't say anything.

Calhoun stood. "Take the bastard and go home. We'll be back for him."

"We leavin'?" Marshall asked eagerly.

"Yep."

The six men began saddling their horses as Templeton walked away, pushing his son ahead of him, cursing a blue streak. Dewey was trying to convince his father that he did not hate him.

Calhoun and the others pulled out soon afterward, crossing Clear Creek and then cutting southeast until they hit the stage road. They trotted down the well-marked slash across the rolling Texas prairie. They stopped only once.

Shortly after dawn, Marshall spotted the stage coming toward them from the south. They stopped and pulled their guns. The stage pulled to a halt.

"Don't get nervous with that scattergun, Fred," Calhoun said.

Waverly recognized him. "Calhoun? What're you doin' out here holdin' up the stage? You're supposed to be lookin' for horse thieves."

"I am."

"Huh?"

Calhoun pointed his Dragoon at Endicott. "Get down, Charlie," he ordered.

"What's this all about?" Endicott asked.

Calhoun cocked the revolver. "Get down."

Endicott wrapped the reins around the brake handle and began climbing down.

A passenger stuck his head out the window. "Hey, what's the problem out there?" he asked, voice agitated.

Marshall turned to him and said harshly, "Get your head back inside, mister, before I put a bullet in it."

At the same time, Endicott's feet hit the ground. He noted that Calhoun's attention was distracted however momentarily, and he went for his gun.

Calhoun shot Endicott in the shoulder. Endicott dropped the revolver. Then Calhoun shot him again, this time in the left leg. Endicott fell. Calhoun swung his pistol back toward Waverly, just in case.

The stage guard was just sitting there, shotgun across his lap. "You mind explainin' what's goin' on, Mister Calhoun?" he asked politely.

"Charlie's mixed up with Alexander's gang of outlaws, who're the ones been stealin' the horses and mules."

"You sure?" Waverly asked skeptically.

Calhoun nodded. "Templeton's son was involved, too. He'd pass word to Alexander through Charlie."

"If you say so." Waverly was still skeptical.

"Don't believe him, Fred!" Endicott bellowed. "Goddamn lyin' son of a bitch."

Marshall dismounted and kicked Endicott in the side as he lay on the ground. "Alexander and his scum rode through Boggy Hollow a few days ago. Killed a bunch of good people. He ain't gettin' away with it. And neither are you." He was giving his newfound hatred of white men free rein.

"But I . . ."

"Shut up!" Calhoun roared. "Lyin' your ass off ain't gonna get you out of this one, you festerin' bag of shit."

Waverly watched the exchange, and could see the truth on all the faces involved. He remembered a few things—little things here and there—that Endicott had done that hadn't made sense to him. But with this new information, they made sense now.

"I believe you, Calhoun," he said. "But how the hell'm I supposed to get back to Cross River now? I got no driver."

"I can drive that rig," Abe Johnson said.

Calhoun nodded. "Somebody wrap rags or somethin' on Endicott's wounds. Then truss him up good and tight and throw him in the coach." While that was going on, Calhoun looked at Waverly. "When you stop at Templeton's station, tie up Dewey and haul him back to Cross River with you, too."

Waverly nodded. "What do I do with 'em when I get 'em there?"

"Have Lewis lock 'em up. Tell him and Ferguson that I'll be back as soon as I can with Alexander and any of the others I get. You can also tell them that if they try to lock me up again—or if they let Endicott and Templeton go—I'll kill 'em both."

Waverly raised his eyebrows and whistled, but he said nothing.

Calhoun moved off to be by himself. He waited, impatient to be on the way. He used the time to reload his Colt. It was only a few minutes before Endicott was in the stagecoach, Johnson's horse was tied to the back, and Johnson was in the driver's seat. Then Calhoun and the others galloped off.

By late afternoon, they rode into Sharp Bend, which sat near the north bank of the Brazos River, in the sharp bend of the river. It looked much like Cross River, though perhaps a bit smaller.

The five men were conscious of the stares they received, but they ignored them, other than to keep a wary eye out for danger. They stopped in front of the Butterfield stage office, and Calhoun dismounted. He walked inside.

Jason Billings, the man in charge, glanced up. He looked puzzled a moment, then remembered. "You're

Mister Calhoun, aren't you? The one Mister Ferguson hired to catch the horse thieves."

Calhoun nodded. He had been here once before, when he had first taken the job.

"Had any luck?"

"I know who they are and generally where they are."

"Oh?" Billings said, interested. "Who and where?"

"Micah Alexander. He's supposed to . . ."

"He's in Sharp Bend," Billings said.

Calhoun nodded again. "I know that. What I don't know is where in Sharp Bend."

"Try Finnegan's saloon. Eighth Street. Down the street out here, third left. It's about half-block down on the left."

Calhoun nodded.

"You got help?" Billings asked, concerned. "Alexander's got a dozen men or so with him."

"I got help." He nodded thanks and headed outside. Without a word, he mounted up and trotted off, the Choctaws at his side. He found the bar with no trouble and they all dismounted.

Calhoun pushed through the saloon doors first. Marshall and Franklin were half a step behind, and Grant and Jefferson the same space behind them. Calhoun stopped just inside and looked around.

"Hey, get them goddamn Injins outta my saloon," the bartender shouted.

Calhoun ignored him, still looking around. Then he spotted Alexander, who was at a table near the back with thirteen men gathered at his and two other tables. A number of prostitutes were with the men.

"Hey!" the bartender shouted again. "Get them goddamn stinkin' Injins outta my saloon!"

Calhoun calmly drew one of the Dragoons with his left hand and fired at the bartender, who had pulled out a scattergun. He dropped the shotgun and fell against the back bar and then to the floor when the ball punched through his chest. Glass shattered.

Saloon patrons looked up in surprise and fear. None could flee, since Calhoun and the four Choctaws were still standing in the doorway, so they took refuge behind the bar, or upturned tables.

Calhoun pointed and then began walking toward the back of the saloon, spurs jingling softly. As he walked, he pulled his other Colt. When Calhoun and the Choctaws were halfway across the saloon, Alexander and his men opened fired.

So did Calhoun and the Choctaws. The Indians dove for cover as patrons headed for the door. Calhoun stayed upright, walking calmly and firing steadily. Bullets tugged at his shirt and sent his hat flying, but still he walked on straight.

Several outlaws were shot down; others began running. Suddenly Alexander and four of his men bolted through a doorway to the back. Moments later, another one made it. The few left behind were slowly shot down.

Calhoun ran out of ammunition in his Dragoons and dropped them back into their holsters. He pulled the pistol he had taken from Marshal Lewis and fired until that was dry, too.

Silence swept over the saloon, except for the drip of whiskey, and the occasional clatter as another piece of glass fell.

Calhoun moved forward, empty pistol in hand. He kicked or turned over with his boot each outlaw he came to. All were dead. He set a table and chair upright and then sat down. He patiently reloaded all three pistols, figuring he would need them soon.

Marshall came up and got another chair. He, too, began reloading. "Ray and Johnny're dead," he said flatly.

Calhoun nodded. He could do nothing to bring them back to life, and he didn't know them enough to want to grieve over them.

"I'd like to get them back home to Boggy Hollow so we can bury them."

Calhoun nodded again.

"You gonna come along?"

"Nope."

"We won't go through Cross River," he said. "We'll leave the stage road before then and cut cross country to the Red."

"I'll ride with you that far." He stood. "Now let's move."

"We're tired, Wade," Marshall said, also standing. "We can use some sleep."

"I know. But I don't want Alexander gettin' too big a jump on me this time. Besides, you think the law's gonna let us stay the night peacefully in Sharp Bend?"

"Reckon not." He nodded, mind made up. "We'll leave as soon as we can get the bodies on their horses."

"We'll stop somewhere outside of Sharp Bend and camp."

"Good."

"But I still plan to be back on the trail before dawn. You ain't ready, I'll go on without you."

Marshall nodded.

CHAPTER

* 21 *

Calhoun found Will Templeton standing in a hole, busily throwing dirt with an old shovel. His face was coated with tears and snot, and he was babbling incoherently. Calhoun stopped his horse and sat watching, and listening.

Templeton was not aware of his visitor. He just kept slinging dirt and ranting quietly: "Goddamn son of a bitch . . . murderin' bastard . . . goddamn . . . gone . . . All gone . . ."

Calhoun moved up to where Templeton could see him and dismounted. Calhoun looked at Templeton, shocked.

"They killed her," Templeton blathered. He swiped a hand across his face, smearing snot and tears even more.

"Who?"

"Elva. They killed Elva." Choking sobs racked Templeton's big shoulders.

"Who killed her?" Calhoun got a chill down his spine.

"Alexander."

"When? How?"

"Before . . . I don't know . . . she's gone . . ."

Calhoun grabbed Templeton by the shirtfront and shook him hard. "Goddammit, calm down and tell me what happened!" he shouted.

Templeton blinked a few times and the fresh tears stopped. He looked as if he had just come out of a trance.

Calhoun released his shirt. "What happened?" he asked.

Templeton jabbed the shovel into the mound of dirt and sat on the edge of the grave he was digging. "Alexander and four, five other men rode in here. Early today. They were lookin' for Dewey, that little bastard." Templeton's words had turned suddenly harsh.

Calhoun handed him a cigarette he had just rolled and lit, then began making another for himself.

Templeton nodded thanks and wiped his face with a bandanna. He shoved the bandanna away and puffed a few moments. "Dewey wasn't here. The stage come by yesterday and picked him up. Fred Waverly told me you told him to do it." He looked at Calhoun in question.

Calhoun nodded.

"Alexander was in a piss-poor humor when he got here, and got even worse when he found out about Dewey. He started slappin' Elva around, and I tried to stop him. He knocked me out. When I woke up, I found . . . she was . . ." A great, racking sob tore out of him. He brought himself under control with an effort. "They'd killed her. Shot her to pieces."

Templeton quieted and smoked on his cigarette for a bit. Calhoun was eager to get going, a sense of urgency clutching at him, but he forced himself to wait patiently.

"Why'd they do that, Mister Calhoun?" Templeton suddenly asked, face pained once again.

Calhoun shrugged. "Some men're like that," he said lamely. He paused. "Alexander and the others headed for Cross River, I reckon?" he asked. He felt sure that Alexander would want to get to the town to either rescue Dewey Templeton, or kill the young man so he couldn't testify at a trial. Calhoun was surprised when Templeton shook his head.

"Nope," Templeton said. "They rode northwest out of here."

Another chill swept up Calhoun's back. "You sure?" he asked harshly.

"Yes, I'm sure," Templeton said with a curt nod. "I figure they were afraid to go to Cross River."

"Shit," Calhoun breathed. He jumped into the saddle in a single leap and spurred his horse into a run, mind beset by worries. He and the two Choctaws had gone their separate ways earlier in the day, with the Indians heading northwest toward the Red River and Boggy Hollow beyond, taking the bodies of their two friends home for burial, and Calhoun heading for Cross River, figuring Alexander would be heading there. Now he figured there was a good chance Marshall and Tom Grant might run into Alexander and his men or, worse, be ambushed by them.

Throughout the long afternoon, he kept the horse at a good pace, covering ground in a rush, but never really fast enough to suit him. He got to the Red sometime after midnight, and ran the pinto across it. With his poor luck with horses, he very easily could've lost the animal to quicksand, but he did not care. He figured the risk was worth it.

An hour and a half later, he spotted a small fire in the distance, and he pulled up. He moved ahead slowly then, not wanting to run into the outlaws without knowing about it. Then he realized it was the Choctaws.

"Get up," he snapped, walking through the camp. "Come on you lazy bastards, get up!"

Grant and Marshall came awake in a rush, hands darting for pistols.

"Come on, goddammit, time to move," Calhoun said.

"What's wrong with you?" Marshall asked grumpily. He shoved his pistol away and stood. "It's the middle of the night."

"Alexander killed Elva Templeton and then come this way. I think he's headin' for that canyon he's used as his hideout."

"So?" Marshall didn't see any importance to that. "We can run him down soon enough."

"Boggy Hollow's between here and there, and Alexander's one angry son of a bitch at me—and you."

"Goddamn!" Marshall breathed. He looked at Grant and ran off a few phrases in Choctaw.

Both Indians raced to get their horses saddled. Calhoun loosened his saddle, giving the pinto a chance to breath for the first real time in hours. Then he poured himself a cup of coffee and gulped it down. There were beans sitting in the frying pan from the night before, and he wolfed those down, too.

While Calhoun ate and the Choctaws worked, Marshall asked, "What makes you think he's headin' for that canyon?"

"Only place he can get supplies, I figure. Mostly ammunition and food. He'll be afraid to go to Cross River. Once he's resupplied, though, he'll probably run for Arkansas or Missouri."

By the time Calhoun finished his hasty meal, Marshall and Grant were ready. Calhoun hastily tightened his saddle, while Marshall kicked dirt over the fire, including the coffeepot and frying pan.

"I'll lead," Marshall said as he jumped into the saddle. "Let Tom bring up the rear. That way you won't get lost in the dark. He'll have the horses with the bodies of Johnny and Ray." He did not wait for an answer from Calhoun. He just raced off.

Calhoun was not about to argue. The Choctaws knew this land far better than he did, even as much as he had traveled it lately. He just followed the dark shadow of Marshall and his horse.

They thundered into Boggy Hollow just after noon and pulled to a short, dusty stop at Jackson's house. The town had an eerie air to it, as if the place were devoid of humans. A few people looked out their doors or windows and then ventured out tentatively.

Zach Marshall's wife, Charlotte, stepped out, her face twisted in pain and sorrow. Marshall slid off his horse and embraced her, questioning her in their language, softly at first, then more harshly as she hesitated.

Charlotte finally answered, voice broken by sobs and grief.

"Jesus, Tom, what the hell's gone on?" Calhoun asked Grant, who was mounted and sitting next to Calhoun. He looked at Grant. He, too, looked grief stricken. "Translate for me, goddammit!" Calhoun snapped.

"Alexander and his men went through here again," Grant said in a bile-laced voice. "Couple of hours ago. They killed a couple of people, and . . . they carried Winona off with them."

"Shit," Calhoun snarled. "Which way'd they go?"

Grant interrupted Marshall's conversation with Charlotte with the question. Then he turned and pointed north.

Calhoun jerked his horse's head around viciously, and spurred the pinto. He raced off, ignoring the sudden shouts from Marshall and Grant. The two Choctaws caught up to him within minutes, though, as Calhoun regained some of his sense and slowed the pinto a little. Riding the animal to death now wouldn't do a damn thing to help Winona.

An hour later, Calhoun jerked his reins so hard that the pinto almost sat in trying to stop. Calhoun was off the horse before it had even settled, and moving into the brush along the thin trail. He knelt next to Winona's body and turned her gently face up.

Alexander had used a knife on her, and there wasn't much of her body that wasn't carved up. He hadn't spent too much time at it, either, nor had he finished his grisly work very long ago.

Calhoun knelt for a full two minutes, rage rippling through his veins like a writhing nest of snakes. He was even unaware of Marshall kneeling next to him.

The Choctaw's face was flat and blank, and his dark eyes swam with the welling up of his grief. His body was stiff, muscles involuntarily bunching in anger and sorrow.

Calhoun finally stood, aware now of Marshall. "Take her back to Boggy Hollow," he ordered, heading for his horse.

"No!" When Calhoun stopped and turned to face him, Marshall said, "I'm going, too."

"This's my business," Calhoun snapped.

"She was my daughter," Marshall said flatly. When

Calhoun hesitated, Marshall laid a hand on his pistol butt. "Killin' another white man here and now won't bother me." His voice was flat and deadly. "Especially an Indian-hatin' one."

Calhoun took only a moment to decide. He was not afraid of Marshall, and knew that even with Marshall's hand on his revolver, he could still take Marshall down without much effort. But the Choctaw was right. Winona was his daughter, and it was his right to go after Alexander.

Calhoun nodded. "Just me and you," he said flatly.

Marshall nodded and turned. "Tom, please see to Winona for me," he asked softly.

"Go," Grant said quietly. "I'll see to things. Go and kill the white enemies."

Then Calhoun and Marshall were galloping down the trail again, pushing the horses to the limit. They were not even sure how long it took them, but they eventually raced into the gentle box canyon. A hundred yards from the tents, they pulled to a stop and dismounted, Calhoun pulling the Walkers from the saddle holsters.

As the two walked toward the tents, where they could see the outlaws waiting, Calhoun said, "Alexander's mine." Marshall started to argue but Calhoun cut him off. "I want him alive to take him back to Cross River."

"I just want to kill the bastard," Marshall snarled.

"I thought the Choctaws were peaceable people," Calhoun said.

"We are, but when the time to fight does come, we can be some mean sons of bitches. That white bastard is mine."

"I'll kill you first, you red-skinned son of a bitch," Calhoun snarled. "Alexander's going to die, and painfully. After I get him back to Cross River to explain his sins to everyone."

The two men looked at each other, their hatred for their opposite race renewed.

"You promise you'll kill him?" Marshall asked.

Calhoun nodded.

"I still don't like white men."

"I still hate Indians."

"Let's go," Marshall said.

The two turned and started walking toward the seven men who waited for them. "You can have the Choctaw," Marshall said, pointing to an Indian standing with the outlaws.

"Know him?"

"Yep. Orville Catcher. He's from Boggy Hollow. I don't know what he's doin' here, but I never did trust that son of bitch."

At twenty yards, Calhoun fired one of the Walkers. Catcher went down, but started getting back up as his companions began firing. Calhoun plugged him again and then again. Catcher went down to stay.

As at the saloon in Sharp Bend, Calhoun could feel bullets tugging at his clothes, and once one singed his ribs, but he was oblivious to it all. He noted that Marshall wasn't flinching either.

Calhoun shot Alexander in the right shoulder where it connected to the arm. The bullet knocked him down. Calhoun figured the outlaw leader would be unable to do anything for a while, so he turned his attention to the others. But every time Alexander tried to get up, Calhoun would wing a shot just past his head, and the outlaw leader would duck.

Marshall and Calhoun stopped at ten yards from where the outlaws had tried to make their stand. Calhoun dropped the one Walker, which was empty now. The three outlaws who were not down were fleeing. Calhoun drilled one in the back, punching him forward.

Another managed to get on his horse and was racing for the canyon mouth. Calhoun dropped to one knee, Walker extended at arm's length, swinging along, leading the rider. Calhoun fired and the man went sailing off the far side of his horse.

Calhoun dropped the second Walker, now almost empty, and grabbed a Dragoon from the holster. He turned back, but there was little more for him to do. Marshall had taken care of them all—except for Alexander.

Calhoun walked up to Alexander and kicked him in the side when Alexander tried to raise a revolver with his shattered right arm. Calhoun knelt. "What was that goddamn Choctaw doin' here?" he asked.

"Who? Orville?" Alexander tried to laugh but didn't do too well with it. "He's been one of my boys for a spell. When he heard what happened down in Sharp Bend," Alexander spit angrily, "he decided to come with us."

"Why'd you take the woman?" Calhoun asked tightly.

"Get back at you," Alexander said flatly. "Orville told me you'n her were cozy."

"We were, you shit-humpin' son of a bitch."

Alexander looked up into Calhoun's eyes in fear.

Calhoun stood. "Get up," he ordered.

*   *   *

Calhoun looked like hell—and felt worse—when he walked into Henry Ferguson's office in Cross River, shoving Micah Alexander ahead of him. Calhoun had had little sleep since he had left the camp with the Choctaws near Sharp Bend five days ago, plus he had not shaved nor washed. He was filthy, and his clothes pocked with bullet holes. He had ridden back to Boggy Hollow with Marshall, but then left the Choctaw and kept on riding. Neither he nor Marshall had made any professions of friendship for the other.

"Here's your goddamn horse thief, you fat sack of shit," Calhoun snarled, pushing Alexander into a chair. He went and uncorked a bottle of rye and was about to pour some in a glass when he shrugged and just tilted the bottle to his mouth. When he set the bottle down, he rolled a cigarette. Smoking, he leaned back against the wall, feeling the tiredness in his muscles, and the gritty sandiness in his eyes.

He looked from Ferguson to Lewis, who was standing next to Ferguson's desk. "You still got Dewey and Charlie over in the jail, Marshal?" he asked.

Lewis nodded tightly.

"Explain everything to these gentlemen, Mister Alexander," Calhoun said gruffly.

"Piss off," Alexander snapped.

Calhoun came off the wall and punched Alexander in the wounded shoulder as hard as he could.

Alexander screamed, then grunted as his chair fell over and he hit the floor. Calhoun set the chair back up and then dragged Alexander up and into it. "Talk," he commanded. Then he went back to lean against the wall.

Alexander shivered as he remembered the look in Calhoun's flat, deadly eyes, and figured he'd be far better off talking. So he talked, steadily, for more than an hour. Finally, though, he came to a stop.

"Good work, Mister Calhoun," Ferguson said, sounding friendlier than he had in a long time.

"You owe me a fifteen hundred dollars," Calhoun said flatly.

Ferguson gulped and nodded.

"Now," Calhoun said.

Ferguson looked at him in surprise, nodded again and walked to the small safe along the wall under the window. He extracted some money and handed it to Calhoun. As he sat, Ferguson said, "Marshal, would you escort Mister Alexander to the jail. We'll hold the trial as soon as we can."

"There ain't gonna be no trial," Calhoun growled.

"What?" Ferguson asked, swinging around to gape at Calhoun.

"Some crimes need a payin' back in kind," Calhoun said, straightening away from the wall. He pulled his bowie knife. "You like to use knives, don't you, Alexander?" he asked.

Alexander urinated in his pants.

Lewis came around the desk. "Here now, Mister Calhoun, you can't . . ." He stopped when Calhoun smashed him a good shot in the mouth with his left fist.

"Both of you sit!" Calhoun ordered. Then he went to work on Alexander with the knife, heedless of Alexander's screams as well as Ferguson's ineffectual bleatings. It took Alexander almost as long to die as he had talked. And by then, both Ferguson and Lewis had vomited several times, and were cowering in corners.

Calhoun finally pulled a bandanna from his pocket and wiped the blade off. He put the knife away, turned and headed for the door. There was an audience outside. A few of the more intrepid souls had watched Calhoun through a window and kept the others apprised of what was going on. Now the audience looked at him with horror.

Calhoun spotted Irene McGowan. She was clutching Alvin Webb tightly and looking at Calhoun with revulsion. He touched the brim of his hat in her direction. Then he mounted the pinto and rode off.

CLINT HAWKINS is the pseudonym of a newspaper editor and writer who lives in Phoenix, Arizona.

Saddle-up to these